CUMBRIA LIBRARIES

KT-178-053

3 8003 04118 7618

COCKERMOUTH		
0 3 AUG 2022		

County Council

cumbria.gov.uk/libraries

Library books and more......

C.L. 18F

24 hour Renewals 0303 333 1234

SPECIAL MESSAGE TO READERS

THE ULVERSCROFT FOUNDATION
(registered UK charity number 264873)

was established in 1972 to provide funds for research, diagnosis and treatment of eye diseases. Examples of major projects funded by the Ulverscroft Foundation are:-

- The Children's Eye Unit at Moorfields Eye Hospital, London
- The Ulverscroft Children's Eye Unit at Great Ormond Street Hospital for Sick Children
- Funding research into eye diseases and treatment at the Department of Ophthalmology, University of Leicester
- The Ulverscroft Vision Research Group, Institute of Child Health
- Twin operating theatres at the Western Ophthalmic Hospital, London
- The Chair of Ophthalmology at the Royal Australian College of Ophthalmologists

You can help further the work of the Foundation by making a donation or leaving a legacy. Every contribution is gratefully received. If you would like to help support the Foundation or require further information, please contact:

THE ULVERSCROFT FOUNDATION
The Green, Bradgate Road, Anstey
Leicester LE7 7FU, England
Tel: (0116) 236 4325
website: www.foundation.ulverscroft.com

BLUE PERIL

Complicit in Doctor Brooking's efforts to create a monster, Gregory Conrad is ultimately forced to make the main contribution himself, losing his life in the process. However, Brooking discovers that the thing his genius has brought to life possesses a will of its own, as well as superhuman powers . . . Jerry Tern, an investigative reporter, and Vivienne Conrad, Gregory's sister, join forces to investigate her brother's disappearance, but soon become captives of the monster — the so-called Blue Peril of the popular press — and witness at first hand its reign of terror . . .

DENIS HUGHES

BLUE PERIL

Complete and Unabridged

LINFORD
Leicester

First published in Great Britain

First Linford Edition
published 2017

Copyright © 1952 and 2016 by
the Estate of Denis Hughes
All rights reserved

A catalogue record for this book is available
from the British Library.

ISBN 978–1–4448–3346–1

Published by
F. A. Thorpe (Publishing)
Anstey, Leicestershire

Set by Words & Graphics Ltd.
Anstey, Leicestershire
Printed and bound in Great Britain by
T. J. International Ltd., Padstow, Cornwall

This book is printed on acid-free paper

1

Man on the Run

He moved like a ghost from shadow to shadow, dodging between the doorways, avoiding every patch of light that he could. It was one thing to escape from a police net, another to keep clear altogether. Half an hour ago he thought he'd made it, then the whistles had shrilled again. He felt like a man against the world, a hunted man, which was exactly what he was. And the hunt was not far behind. With any luck, he might still reach Brooking's place. That was what he wanted more than anything else. Brooking had landed him in this position; the man could get him out of it. If he didn't . . . But there were ways of making a man do something he didn't want to do.

From somewhere behind him came the whine of a car engine. He ducked into a doorway, standing with his back to the door, holding his breath. They were closer than he'd thought. His legs ached with running; his nerves made him unsteady. Had there been sufficient light, anyone could have seen the gleam of fear and desperation in his eyes. But there was not enough light, and no one to see. Not yet . . .

The car, a black flying squad saloon, tore past. He caught a glimpse of the peaked caps inside; the tense features of the men who hunted him. Then the car was gone and the man in the doorway moved. He didn't have far to go now. Surely they wouldn't be watching the lab. Weeks had passed since the woman had died there. Weeks during which he had relied on Vivienne for concealment. She'd been the only one who believed him innocent, bless her. But he couldn't involve her any longer. It wasn't fair, not with things as they were. No, Brooking was the man to deal with . . .

Panting for breath, he turned the corner. The pool of light from a street lamp fell full on his face for an instant. He was pale and drawn-looking, distracted by the days and nights of suspense and incipient horror. Even the soft felt hat pulled right down over his forehead failed to hide the signs; they were deeply printed in his whole bearing, the hunch of his shoulders, the furtive glance backwards.

When he reached the big building that housed the research laboratory, he paused for a full minute, probing the shadows, seeking anxiously for signs of a watcher. There were none.

Using his own key — that key with which he had let himself in every morning for four long years when he worked with Brooking — he opened the door and slipped inside.

The little reception hall was dark and silent, chilly with the cold of night and bad central heating. He moved quietly down the hallway, knowing exactly where he was going: through a glass door at the end and up a straight flight of stairs. They were lino-covered, brass-nosed, cold and never very clean. He knew this place well.

Outside in the road, the police car went back the other way, moving more slowly. They were combing the district of course.

He was lucky to have got this far so easily.

At the top of the stairs, it was another world into which he stepped. At the end of a spotless white corridor was a lighted office. Opening off that was the lab. Brooking was working late, just as he had guessed would be the case.

The man in the corridor stared at the streak of light under the office door. Now that he was so near, his nerve began to fail. There'd been so much mental strain these last weeks; he was jittery. Then he thought of Vivienne and found courage again. She hadn't shown any weakness when he begged her to hide him. Even with a murder charge hanging over his head, he was still her brother; that was how she had looked at it.

He walked firmly through the office and gripped the handle of the laboratory door. Faint sounds reached his ears from within. The slow smile of hate that was forming on his lips froze and faded. He turned the handle and flung the door open abruptly.

Brooking was stooped over a bench cluttered with tubes and retorts. The air was thick with the tang of chemicals. Brooking did not believe in fresh air. At the sound of his visitor's entrance he straightened up and swung round quickly, a metal spatula poised in his hand. Suddenly it slid from his fingers, clinking unmusically on the enamel surface of the bench.

'Conrad!' he gasped. 'You!' Conrad moved in and closed the door behind him.

'Yes,' he murmured gently. 'It's me, Brooking. You didn't expect me, did you? You thought I was cowering in some hole like a cornered rat!'

Brooking recovered his composure with an effort. He picked up the spatula from where it had fallen, his eyes not leaving his visitor. 'Aren't you rather a fool to come back?' he said quietly. He was older than Conrad, older by twenty years; grey-faced, grey-haired, not very big or imposing. Even his eyes were grey; a little on the small size, but shrewd and clever for all that, as Conrad knew to his cost. Very, very clever . . .

'I was a fool ever to duck in the first

place,' he replied. 'Better to have brazened it out.'

Brooking smiled. He was quite himself again now. 'You'd have been convicted and hung.'

Conrad moved to the bench, close to Brooking. His eyes swept the big laboratory briefly. At any rate, the thing was not in sight. He was glad of that. 'Hung for something I didn't do,' he whispered grimly. 'You're the foulest of swine, aren't you? Do you think I'd have associated myself with this work of yours if I'd had any inkling of what it would entail?'

Brooking shrugged. 'You were enthusiastic enough at first,' he reminded gently. 'And after all, you must have known we should need living tissue for vital organs, to say nothing of nerve ganglia and suchlike.'

Conrad closed his eyes. It was all too clear in his memory for comfort. He could still see that nameless woman's face when Brooking struck. And he could still see only too clearly the fanatical gleam in Brooking's eyes as he went to work on the still-quivering flesh. Brooking had never flinched. He needed human tissue fresh enough to preserve and form part of the thing; the woman had supplied it.

'I wish I'd never agreed to the work,' said Conrad. 'If I'd had any guts, I'd have told them all about it and cleared myself when you said it was I who killed her.'

Brooking smiled complacently. 'Do you really think they'd have believed you?' he sneered. 'You were seen when you disposed of the remains in the river. Seen and recognised, remember?' He shook his head slowly. 'No, they'd not have believed you. And had you told them of our work, you'd only have been laughed at for your trouble.'

Conrad rammed his hands into his pockets to prevent them from shaking. 'Don't call it *our* work!' he snapped.

Brooking shrugged again. 'Why have you come here?' he demanded abruptly. 'You can see you're not welcome; what do you think the police would do if they knew you were here? I'm surprised you didn't manage to slip out of the country.'

'You've never been hunted by the police!' Conrad retorted. 'I'm here because you can help me. You got me into this mess; you get me out! It wouldn't be difficult with the amount of influence you carry.'

'Even certain friends would shy at the idea of getting a man like you out of the country,' said Brooking. 'You know the name you made for yourself, of course . . . ? The most sadistic killer in the history of crime, they called you. There was so much of that young woman missing when they fished the remains out. But they said it was queer because it hadn't been a sex murder.' He smiled. 'You might even have got away with a plea of insanity, Conrad.'

Conrad clenched his fists till his nails dug deep into his palms. 'You're going to help me, you devil!' he grated. 'If you don't, I'm going to treat you like you treated that woman. You wouldn't like that! You wouldn't like it any more than she did, poor kid.'

Brooking cocked his head to one side. 'It must be a terrible handicap to be sentimental,' he murmured. 'Now I, for instance, never give a thought to what is necessary. Each fresh set of circumstances produces a different problem, you know. There's always a solution to fit. It's only a matter of searching till you find the solution, then you go right in and get to work.'

Conrad succeeded in smiling. 'You always did love to drivel!' he snapped. 'I don't want to listen to your lectures on surmounting obstacles. All I want is for you to get me out of this country and clear away.'

'Obstacles . . . ?' murmured Brooking idly. 'What an apt choice of word.' He frowned, apparently thinking over some obscure problem. Then: 'You wouldn't like to come in with me again, I suppose? The work isn't finished yet . . . I can still use your brain, Conrad. Why not help me again? You could stay concealed in this place for years without ever being found.' His eyes were sharp, bird-like. 'It might be worth it in the long run, you know.'

Conrad thrust his face forward. He was very close to Brooking. 'I'd see you in hell before lifting a finger to further your filthy efforts!' he said.

Brooking said nothing, but his eyes were eloquent. Then: 'A pity,' he murmured. 'I could use your brain, as I say.'

Conrad was still very close to him. Too close . . .

★   ★   ★

The telephone at Police Divisional Headquarters jangled. Detective Inspector 'Happy' Dutch leaned across and lifted the receiver, listening.

A voice said: 'Doctor Brooking here. I've recently had a visit from Gregory Conrad. Yes, Conrad — the wanted man himself, I tell you!' There was a touch of impatience in the voice now. 'Of course he's gone! He made menacing demands of me, then knocked me out. Yes, he was gone when I came to. Several pounds in cash missing, and some clothes as well. He said something about leaving the country . . . You'll be round? By all means. Yes, I was working late in the lab. Of course not! I often work late. Very well, Inspector, I'll be waiting for you. Yes, just come in the front and up the stairs.

10

I've left it unlocked.'

Dutch raised his head, clapped on a big brimmed hat and banged it over his head with the flat of his hand. He glared at the sergeant on the other side of the room.

'They missed Conrad by only a little!' he snapped. 'Been to Brooking's place. Come on, we may pick up a lead from there!'

The car howled through the dark deserted streets. When it screeched to a stop outside the laboratory block, all was quiet.

Happy Dutch opened the car door and got a foot on the pavement. 'You wait here,' he told the sergeant. 'I don't want anyone snooping around till I've heard the yarn.'

The sergeant nodded. Dutch was closing the door when the sound of running footsteps caught his ear. He spun round and stared up the darkened street, eyes narrowed. Then he growled something under his breath as a figure came within his vision.

The figure was out of breath, slightly dishevelled. A snap-brim felt hat obscured part of its face, and the flapping tails of a raincoat made a cloak round its legs.

'Hello there, Dutch!' the man called. 'What's cooking, eh? We serve the public. Murder by night makes news for breakfast. Did you catch up with Conrad?'

Dutch compressed his lips in a thin line. He disliked heartiness at any time, the middle of the night most of all. But he knew what a sticker Tern could be when it came to getting a story. And this young man with the impish grin was Tern.

'You again!' he grunted. 'I've nothing for you! We didn't get Conrad, and by now he'll be miles away. If there is any information for you, the office will give it out in the usual way. Now hop it!'

Tern had his hands in his pockets. He had recovered his breath with surprising speed, and the grin was there in all its disarming humour. 'You can't kid me,' he said. 'If there isn't a story in this, what are you doing outside Brooking's lab? Conrad was connected with him. Conrad was last seen heading in this direction. Now *you're* here! If that doesn't smell like a net full of clues, I'll never write another word!'

The inspector eyed him sourly in the dim light. 'There's nothing for you,' he repeated. 'I'm here on business.' He jerked his head to the sergeant, now standing by the car. 'See Mister Tern doesn't interfere,' he said grimly.

Tern grinned a shade more widely. 'I'll be very good, I promise, Inspector,' he said. 'Let me come and see the mysterious Brooking with you. Be a pal and give me a break, can't you?'

Dutch ignored him, turning his back and going in through the door of the block. Tern found the attentive sergeant right beside him.

'The inspector meant that,' he murmured. 'You'll get no story tonight, son.'

Tern pulled a wry face, then shrugged his shoulders inside his raincoat. 'So it seems,' he grunted. 'Oh well . . . I'll be around first thing in the morning, Sergeant.'

He turned away and walked dejectedly down the street. But his expression was far from dejected. There was something moving in the Conrad affair, he was sure of that — and if only he could get the story . . . With Jerry Tern, the accurate reporting of news was almost a religion.

An alleyway went down off the street about a hundred yards from where he had left the police car. He glanced back, then ducked into it and started running. The alley joined another one running at right angles to it. Tern paused and listened, glancing about to get his bearings. A lighted window further down gave him the rough location of the block he wanted. The alley backed it.

A storage yard opened off the alley behind the block. The gate, a not very strong affair, was low enough to climb. Inside the yard was a building abutting the main one. The lighted window looked out on the flat leaded roof. Tern found a packing case and reached the roof, moving towards the window. Through it he stared into an office. There was no one in sight, but he thought he could hear voices seeping through from beyond another door.

'Get myself hung for this!' he grunted, heaving at the window. The lower half went up with a scraping noise after he'd eased the catch back with a knife. Then he swung his leg over the sill and was standing in the office, closing the window quietly behind him. He slipped his torch back in his pocket and tiptoed to the closed door. The other door was open, revealing a long corridor beyond.

Just as he reached the closed door, someone opened it from inside. He was caught now, he thought ruefully. No chance of eavesdropping!

'What the devil do you mean by this?' demanded Dutch. He glared at Tern belligerently. Beyond Dutch was Brooking. Tern ignored the inspector for an instant, taking in the other man. It was the first time he had been face to face with Brooking. What he saw he disliked at once.

'Sorry, Dutch,' he said soberly. 'I had to find out what was going on. The story, you know . . . '

'I'll give you a story!' grunted Dutch. He turned to Brooking. 'This man is a newspaper reporter, sir. You can charge him with unlawful entry if you like. They get too big for their boots sometimes.

Have to curb 'em!'

But Brooking only smiled indulgently. 'Far be it from me to stint news if it's in the public interest,' he said mildly. 'The young man shows remarkable determination in getting in. You left someone on duty, didn't you?'

'I did! How *did* you get in, Tern?'

'I gave the sergeant the slip,' came the answer.

Dutch breathed heavily.

'It wasn't his fault, honestly.'

'Never mind, Inspector,' said Brooking. 'He may as well stay now he's here. As I was just about to explain, this must have been the window Conrad used. When I came to, I found it open.'

'You closed it again?' Dutch's eyebrows arched. Quite plainly he disapproved. But the window was closed.

Jerry Tern held his peace. Something was humming in his brain, but for the moment the significance of it escaped him.

'You were struck on the head, sir?' Dutch said.

Brooking nodded. 'Just there,' he

answered, lowering his skull for inspection.

'A nasty bruise, sir,' murmured Dutch. 'Very nasty.'

They moved to the window through which Conrad was alleged to have made his escape. Outside on the flat lead roof there were no footprints visible.

The inspector clambered out, flashing his torch round. 'A perfect escape route,' he grunted. 'The man might be anywhere by now.' He glanced back at Tern, vaguely suspicious. Tern grinned in the flashlight. He knew now the significance of what had previously escaped him.

Dutch came back off the roof, dusting his hands and closing the window again, snapping the catch across. 'Nothing difficult about getting in this way,' he commented. 'Someone used a knife blade on the catch.'

Tern didn't like the way he said 'someone'. There had been just that shade of accent on the word. Then Dutch was saying: 'Thank you, sir. We'll let you know if there are any developments. Conrad is pretty hard pressed, but I doubt he'll come back again.' He hesitated. 'Keep the doors and windows securely locked in case.' He was moving across the office, heading for the corridor and stairway.

At the top of the flight he turned and shot a glance at Tern. 'You better come with me, young man,' he said grimly. 'A word or two of advice wouldn't come amiss in your case.'

Tern grinned. 'Anything to oblige,' he answered. He nodded affably to Brooking, who smiled a little. The two men went on down the stairs to the front door. Out on the pavement, the sergeant was standing guard. He showed surprise at seeing Tern, as was only natural in a sense.

Tern got ready to run. But the inspector's voice was very gentle. Even his detaining hand was light. 'Now,' he said softly, 'tell me, was that window undone when you got in through it?'

Tern did some rapid thinking. 'No,' he replied. 'I had to use a knife on the catch.'

Dutch's eyes were veiled in the gloom. 'Thanks,' he said. His voice hardened. 'If you pull any more tricks of that sort when I'm around, you can look out for trouble!'

'Okay — that's fair enough,' Tern said. They parted on more or less amicable terms.

The police car was whining away in the distance. For a long ten seconds, Tern stood on the edge of the pavement, watching the red gleam of the tail-lights till they disappeared. Then he turned to the doorway again, reaching for the handle. But Brooking had locked it after their departure. Tern frowned; it would have to be the back window again, he decided. A pity . . .

He started off down the street for the alleyway once more. When he reached the corner and glanced over his shoulder, there was another figure walking down the opposite pavement. He knew that the figure must have stepped from one of the doorways not far from the laboratory entrance. Curious . . .

2

Monstrous Night

Tern knew the other person had not been coming down the street because it had been empty only a few seconds before. Whoever it was just had to have stepped from one of the doorways across the street from Brooking's door. The time was two-thirty a.m. And the hurrying figure was that of a woman. Yes, it was curious, he decided.

He slid down the alleyway and waited just out of sight. A moment or two later, the shadow of the woman fell across the ground, hesitating. Then she turned down in his wake.

'Hello,' said Tern. He flashed his torch full in her face. She gasped and tried to back out quickly. 'Don't go yet, Miss Conrad,' he said. His fingers were tight on her wrist. At the sound of her name, she seemed to stiffen. 'You're looking for your brother, aren't you?' he murmured. 'No, I'm not a policeman. If it's any consolation, he's supposed to have got away.'

He still kept the torch on her face, counting the freckles and thinking that a woman as decent as Vivienne should never have been plagued by trouble of such grim proportions as mixing with murder. But that was life . . .

'He got away?' she breathed. 'Who are you?'

'Jerry Tern,' he answered. 'It's time you went home to bed. Your brother isn't here; I was with the police when Dutch called on Brooking.'

She relaxed a little. He switched off the torch and let her stand away slightly. She shuddered, making a queer little sound in her throat. 'Greg was a fool to walk out,' she said suddenly. 'He — he thought it wasn't fair on me.'

'You've been hiding him, of course. Only natural — especially when you were convinced he wasn't guilty.'

'Of course he wasn't guilty!' she said vehemently. 'Do you think I don't *know* he didn't kill that poor woman?'

'Pity you couldn't have proved it,' said Tern regretfully. 'Come on now, I'll take you home. We can pick up a taxi to share.'

She walked beside him without further persuasion. There was a kind of crushed slant to her shoulders and head when they reached the main road with its brighter lights. He did not break the silence that grew between them. Vivienne had had a tough deal; she deserved something better. Tern remembered her clearly; remembered how she had insisted that her brother could never have killed anyone. Her photo had been on the front page of the yellow press more than once since Conrad disappeared. Sister of the wanted man! And all the time, despite questioning and subtle pressure, she had managed to conceal her brother, convinced he was innocent. Well, he might be for all that.

'He told me such horrible things about Brooking,' she said, breaking in on his thoughts. 'It's all too dreadful to believe, and yet . . . Oh what am I going to do?'

'Tell me about it,' he said. 'I'm the

original answer when it comes to trouble. The perfect substitute for a maiden aunt.' He grinned down at her. 'How did you come to be in this neighbourhood at this particular time?'

'Something Greg mentioned before he slipped away. He said Brooking had got him into this jam, and he was going to make him confess or help him get clear of the country. When I found he'd gone, I came straight here. I was too late because the police were already on the scene. Then I saw you, and you looked suspicious, so I thought I'd follow you.'

'Glad you did. According to your brother, then, the guilty party is Brooking?'

She nodded. A taxi hove in sight down the lighted channel of the road. Tern took Vivienne's arm firmly. She gave an address to the driver.

Tern sat beside her in the darkness of the taxi, thinking. He already knew that Brooking was a liar. If Vivienne was to be believed, he was probably a murderer as well. If there wasn't a story in this he would get himself the sack, but at least he might help her.

Neither of them spoke till the taxi stopped outside a gaunt house in a quiet backwater not far from the city. Tern remembered hearing that the Conrads, brother and sister, had inherited the place from their parents. As they went up the steps to the front door, he noticed that the house was not in very good repair.

'Take a couple of aspirins and go to bed,' he advised. 'I won't come in, but I'll meet you tomorrow morning — this morning, I mean. Where shall it be?'

She regarded him steadily for an instant, then named a place.

The taxi was waiting. 'Just one thing,' Tern said. 'Can you give me any idea in a few words why you think Brooking is the guilty man?'

Her latch key was in the Yale, turning. 'Greg told me something I couldn't believe,' she whispered hesitantly. 'He said that Brooking was a worse monster than the thing they'd been creating between them. That's all I know, and it doesn't make a lot of sense, but . . . Greg said he was keen at first because it was a wonderful thing, but then Brooking killed that woman simply and solely because whatever they were doing needed fresh, living tissue.' Her eyes were wide, full of some nameless horror that defied expression.

Tern's face was grim. He touched her arm gently, reassuringly. 'Go to bed,' he whispered. 'I've a lot of work to do before daylight. See you in the morning, ten o'clock. And thanks for . . . being friendly.'

She stood in the open doorway till the taxi was out of sight, seeing him wave and feeling strangely comforted. Had she known it, she was going to need a considerable amount of comfort before very long. It was just as well that she didn't know.

The taxi carried Tern to Fleet Street, where he paid it off. After the almost deserted streets through which he had come, his office was a hive of activity, contrasting oddly with the secret silence of the things that had gone before.

He wrote up a hurried account of Conrad's movements during the night, ending with a hint that the wanted man would soon be arrested. The sub-editor scanned it, nodded curtly, and glanced up at him. 'Nothing more?' he said.

'Not yet. The night's still young.'

'Something on your mind?'

'Maybe. The web-spinning habits of the spider, for one thing. Worth studying, you know.'

The sub eyed him shrewdly. 'You'll get the weekly zoological column before long,' he grunted.

Tern grinned. He went out and had a cup of coffee, then made his way back to Brooking's neighbourhood. Spiders . . . He thought about spiders a great deal on the way. They wove webs in all sorts of odd places. Across windows, for instance. A web like that would take time to make. No spider could have woven it between the time of Conrad's entry and exit and his own circumspect admission to the laboratory. Therefore, Brooking had been lying to Happy Dutch. Conrad was supposed to have left, but in view of what Tern had learnt from Vivienne, it seemed strangely on the cards that Conrad had not left; that he would, in fact, never leave. Tern meant to find out for sure. He was also very curious about the work Brooking was supposed to be doing. If it entailed the murder of innocent people for the sake of their flesh — which was what Vivienne had implied — then it ought to be examined.

Using the alley approach again, he attempted the office window once more. But the light was out now, and Brooking had apparently jammed the sash so tightly with a wedge that Tern's efforts to enter were defeated. Swearing softly, Tern stood back and examined the rear face of the block more carefully. The window of the laboratory itself was also in darkness, but on the next storey up there was evidence of activity. A big window glowed from within, immediately above the spot where he was standing. And there was a convenient drainpipe.

Clinging precariously, Tern reached the level of the sill over to one side of the window. 'And there I was, upside down with nothing on the clock!' he murmured to himself. 'If I break my ruddy neck doing this, the paper can pay me damages!'

He strained across, twisting like a

monkey. With one hand firm on the drainpipe, he was just able to peer through the window, only to find to his chagrin that his view was sadly restricted, consisting of little more than a section of the floor a few feet across seen through a gap at the side of the plastic curtain. On one edge of the visible zone was the corner of what looked like a large metal tank; on the other he could see a white bench on which gleamed metal instruments and various pieces of scientific paraphernalia. A second lab, in fact, he realised.

Then without any warning the figure of Brooking, white-coated now, came into view. He carried an enamel tray or bowl in his hands, but Tern could not see what it contained. Instead his gaze was riveted on Brooking's hands.

They were stained bright red. And there were smudges of red on his jacket too. The red was the red of human blood.

Tern almost lost his grip on the drainpipe in his efforts to see more of the room. He could just glimpse a chair on which a pile of male clothing had been dumped; and then the scientist occupied his attention again. The man was bending over the tank, the bowl and his hands out of sight as he worked with every indication of feverish haste. His back was to the window, blocking the view.

Tern muttered something uncomplimentary beneath his breath. His hands were aching now. In a moment or two he would have to get a better grip on the pipe and the sill. The muscular strain made his arm quiver violently. But so intense was his interest in what was going on in the room that he hung on grimly. Brooking had straightened up from the tank, wiping his hands on a piece of gauze. The light caught his glasses as he moved. The piece of gauze was red and blotched. Then Brooking walked away and out of range of vision. Tern would have given almost anything to have seen what was in the tank. He could see several insulated wires trailing over the edge of it, but what it held remained a tantalising secret.

He was wondering how to find out more, when the drainpipe gave a grating protest and sagged away from the wall above him. His fingers scrabbled wildly to retain their grip; his heart thudded painfully. Then he was falling as the ruptured pipe described a graceful arc in the darkness.

★   ★   ★

'While it's fresh!' muttered Brooking. 'It must be fresh!' He worked with feverish haste, his hands shaking a little — not with fear or horror at what he was doing, but with nervous tension and sheer fanatical excitement. It was almost done now! A few more minutes, half an hour at the most, and he would know whether or not he had succeeded. No man had ever attempted such a tremendous undertaking before. He would be the first to fashion life with his own amazing skill!

The surgical instruments clicked and flashed in the beam of the powerful arc lamp above his head. All that remained of Gregory Conrad lay stripped on the table, the soft *hiss* of running water washing away the warm blood from Conrad's skull.

The brain was ready for total detachment now. A few deft strokes with a scalpel and the job was done. Brooking could not resist a cynical smile as he raised and transferred the grey mass to a clinical bowl. 'I said I could use your brain, Conrad!' he sneered in a whisper. 'You didn't know what sort of a joke that was, did you?'

Conrad failed to answer. Unconscious till a few moments before, he had now ceased to breathe. Brooking had what he needed for his work. That was all that mattered.

Conrad's brain was a normal one, no bigger or smaller than the brains of millions of other people. Brooking took it across the room to the galvanised tank, passing the chair on which he had tossed his victim's clothing when he stripped his insensible body for the operation. The body would have to be disposed of presently, but that was a simple matter now that he had had time to work out the routine. If Conrad had not returned, Brooking would have been compelled to find some other source of cerebral tissue, hence his readiness on Conrad's timely arrival. Everything had fitted in like a pattern. And now the great work, the miracle of creation, was nearing its ultimate conclusion.

Coupling speed with skill, the scientist placed the brain in its final position. Delicate fibres were joined and sewn, the artificial structure of the bloated skull completed.

Brooking stood back for a moment, examining his handiwork with a critical eye. There was no room for error; even the smallest detail must be perfect. His eyes went from head to toe of the hideously grotesque figure in the tank. It floated sluggishly in a saline solution, the enormous ungainly head supported in a metal crutch. Conrad had never seen this thing at its advanced state of structure; he and Brooking had only been in the initial stages when the need for living tissue arose in the first place. That had been when the woman had died to provide what was needed. But now it was over. Before long, if Brooking's skill had been good enough, the figure would live and breathe, move and perhaps even articulate. The scientist might have to teach it the rudiments of speech, but that would all be part of the work. A feverish eagerness seized him. With the brain cells knitted into the hideous cranium, he could start the energizing process.

The figure bobbed slowly in the saline. From a socket in the centre of its queer, angular metal torso, a pair of wires ran to plug electrodes on either side of the short neck. The arms and legs were fashioned from a blue-coloured plastic substance, but the hands were those of a human being. Red-coloured protective cuffs covered the join between the plastic arms and the figure's wrists, while a brief pair of shorts of the same material protected the hips and groin. But it was the head and features which would have struck terror into the heart of anyone seeing it unexpectedly. That monstrous shiny skull, red-veined and yellowed, was at least four times the size of a normal man's head. The eyes were yellow, dead-looking now, with blank blue irises tinged with red. There were no eyebrows or lashes, and the nose consisted merely of two gaping holes in the centre of the face, below which was a straight cut slit to form the lipless mouth. The whole effect was horrific, yet Brooking fairly crooned over the tank as he put the finishing touches to his masterpiece. Here, he told himself, was true creation, the outcome of months of work, the successful fusing of a robot with living human flesh.

Brooking drew a deep breath and glanced around the lab. Everything was ready. He took off his white coat and slipped on the jacket of his normal suit. A hurried wash at the sink rinsed away the blood from his hands. Then Conrad's mortal remains were wrapped in a sheet and thrust out of sight in the cage of a small lift concealed in the wall of the room. Brooking was ready.

Returning to the galvanised tank, he connected the wires to a power circuit. His hands were unsteady; a beading of sweat stood out on his brow. His fingers closed on a big resistance lever, moving it across its segments with care, a pause between each as the current mounted in pressure. Every nerve in his body tingled as he watched the figure in the tank. A small figure, little bigger than a boy's, with a monstrous head in which a man's brain had but recently been put.

Electrolytic bubbles rose swiftly to the surface of the saline solution. The whole of the liquid content of the tank seemed to vibrate at high frequency. Brooking increased the current still further, his eyes darting to an ammeter on the switchboard beside the rheostat.

Almost before he turned his head again, there was a sudden convulsion in the tank, a gurgle of horrible breath, the vibration of Life itself. The stirring increased so that Brooking uttered a gasp of involuntary fear. But he knew he had succeeded now. The thing was alive! First one hand crept up over the edge of the tank, then it raised itself so that the awful bald skull gleamed wetly in the light.

Slowly at first, then with rapidly increasing strength, it raised itself more and more, turning its head and staring at him with terrible, soulless eyes. Its mouth was working in a jerky fashion, little croaking noises issuing from it.

Brooking released his hold on the switch handle and took a pace towards the tank. His body was shaking so badly with excitement that he could barely stand upright.

The humanesque figure croaked again, moving with clumsy stiffness till it stood on the floor in front of him, head back, staring at him with its hostile eyes.

'Welcome to Life!' said Brooking. He had to lick his lips before he could frame the words, so dry had his mouth become.

'Life?' echoed the figure. Its voice was thin, a shrill piping sound, incredible to Brooking's ears. 'You gave me life, did you? You made me!'

Brooking was suddenly and unaccountably afraid. He had brought this thing to life, yet had not expected it to talk and reason on its own. 'Why do you say that?' he stammered. 'How did you know I made you?'

The thing did not answer at once, but started walking up and down the length of the room, strutting like a mechanical toy. At the far end of the room it came to a halt and whirled about with unexpected swiftness.

'I know everything!' it snapped peevishly. 'I know whose clothes those are on the chair; I know what's in that hidden lift cage. I know a lot that would surprise you, Brooking. Now that you've brought me to life, you shall suffer for it!' In a swift leap it sprang onto the bench, lightly and easily, to stand there pointing an accusing finger at Brooking.

Brooking cowered away, terrified of what he had done. But the shrill voice only went on and on till he barely listened to what it was saying. And with every second his fear increased, because he knew now that what he had fashioned with his own hands was a foul and vindictive creature of darkness, more dangerous than any human being, more of a peril to himself than Gregory Conrad had ever been. Yet this was Conrad's revenge, for Conrad's brain was in this monster.

3

The Peril Strikes

Jerry Tern fell awkwardly, although the drop itself was not tremendous. His right leg was shot through with burning fire as he landed on the lead roof, then the length of drainpipe struck him a violent blow on the back of his head and he lost interest. He remembered feeling vaguely surprised that the din of his crash had not roused the entire neighbourhood, Brooking included. In actual fact, however, the breaking of the drainpipe and the noises that followed had not been overly loud. The lead roof on which he landed gave only a dull thud on impact, and up in the laboratory on the second floor Brooking was so deeply absorbed in his work that he noticed nothing unusual.

When Tern opened his eyes, however, he was not alone. In the gloom a large shape bulked beside him, the sound of its breathing heavy in the silence. He tried to shift himself, but the stabbing pain in his right leg reminded him forcibly of preceding events. The shape beside him gave a grunt.

'See what comes of snooping?' it said. 'Why you chaps can't leave it to the police, I don't know. No, don't try to move; you might have broken something important.'

Tern gritted his teeth, peering sideways and upwards. 'Hiya, Dutch,' he muttered. 'You would be the one to find me in this position! What gives?'

Inspector Dutch sat back on his heels, tipping his hat forward a shade and cocking an eyebrow towards the lighted window above them. 'That's just what I'm going to ask you, son,' he murmured. 'Better get you down first. Take it easy.'

Tern shook some of the ache out of his head and eased himself to a sitting position, flexing his right leg with the utmost care. It hurt like the devil, but wasn't broken.

'I'll make it,' he whispered grimly. 'Just a twist, that's all.' With the inspector's assistance he reached the edge of the roof and lowered himself over, feeling with his feet for the packing crate below. In a moment or two he was sitting on the ground with his back against the store-shed and the bulk of Dutch alongside him in the shadows. The pain in his leg decreased; his head still ached where the broken pipe had caught it.

'Look, Tern,' said Dutch, 'I don't know what you've been up to, but you'd better not conceal any evidence — it's a grave offence.'

Tern thought quickly. 'Like getting in through a window and not telling anyone about the spider's web, eh?' he said.

'Something like that,' grunted Dutch. 'Conrad didn't use that window, did he? You knew that.'

'When I went through it, there was a darned great web all over one corner of the lower sash. I saw it in the flashlight beam, so I know. No one has used that window for a long time before me. Spiders aren't that quick!' He eyed his companion keenly, trying to read his expression in the darkness, and failing. 'You guessed there was something fishy in Brooking's story?'

Dutch nodded. 'That's why I'm here. You've been up to that window, I take it? What did you see?'

'Another lab,' answered Tern thoughtfully. 'Several other things, too. Pile of male clothing on a chair, some blood, a lot of paraphernalia that didn't mean much, and our friend Brooking.' He turned impulsively, gesturing with a rueful grin. 'Look, Dutch, get inside that building and work on the swine! I can't tell you everything yet, but there's more nasty things going on in there than I like to think about. Briefly, it's my bet that Conrad never left this building; that Brooking killed him because he knew too much and threatened him with exposure. There's something fiendish cooking, I tell you, with Brooking stirring the pot.'

Dutch nodded curtly. 'I suffer from roughly the same ideas,' he admitted. 'But thanks for the tip anyway.'

Tern grinned. 'You might not have got it if I hadn't pranged,' he said. 'What are you aiming to do?'

Dutch considered briefly. 'I have a

search warrant,' he admitted. 'As a matter of fact, I was snooping myself when I found you up there. You say the window's fixed so it can't be opened? Never mind. You stay where you are. When I've seen Brooking and taken a look round I'll get an ambulance — or take you home in the car.'

Tern said nothing, only grunted. He was wondering if he could walk on his own. It was sickening to be stuck like this with so much going on. Then Dutch was moving away in the gloom and he was left alone in the yard at the rear of the block.

He waited till Dutch had disappeared, then hoisted himself to his feet. A little experiment showed that he could walk, slowly and painfully. He decided that he must have torn a muscle in his thigh. But at any rate he wasn't completely immobilised, which was something to be thankful for.

It seemed to take hours to reach the end of the alley and start up the other one to the road. By now, he thought, Dutch must have entered the block and discovered what was going on. He cursed his luck again and again. Every inch was a physical effort.

And then from the direction of the laboratory building came the most appalling human scream Tern had ever listened to. It was muffled by walls and windows, but clearly audible. And it was followed almost immediately by the sound of breaking glass, a thin tinkle in the distance.

Tern hurried on, his mouth a tight line from pain and excitement. What the devil was Dutch up to? But when he reached the end of the alley and peered round into the road, he was surprised to see that the inspector was still out in the street, standing back a little, looking upwards. Down the road a black saloon was parked, its lights out. The nearest street lamp cast a sickly glow on the pavement, glinting on broken glass from the front of an upstairs window.

Dutch shouted something upwards. Tern started down the road, heading towards him. Then from inside the block there came another scream of fear and agony mingled. It ended in a horrible choking sound. Tern's breath came swiftly.

'Can't get in!' Dutch yelled, catching sight of him. 'Got to break the door open!'

Before Tern could answer, and while he still had twenty yards to cover, there was a violent eruption of breaking glass from an upper window. Next instant a grotesque figure landed on the pavement, bouncing lightly, whirling as Dutch lunged forward. Tern witnessed the brief encounter: saw the police officer towering over the extraordinary figure; saw Dutch suddenly crash to the ground and lie still. The figure glanced round, then darted away with amazing speed, to be lost in the darkness.

Tern, cursing wildly, staggered forward. He could not shake off the feeling that he had just seen a figure from some nightmare world. No human being could have as enormous a head as the one he had seen on the boy-sized body. He was horrified, shattered by the swiftness of the apparition and the terrible way in which Happy Dutch had measured his length.

The parked police car sprang into life, speeding down the street. Tern called on his last reserves and reached the side of the fallen man just as the car skated to a halt in the road. Dutch was lying unpleasantly still, his face to the night, his hat in the gutter. There was blood on his skull where the glow of the street lamp caught it.

A police whistle shrilled further up the road, and another car whined into motion. The thud of running footsteps added to the general confusion. Here and there lights sprang into being along the darkened street. Someone called out a question that was never answered.

Tern glanced up at the sergeant as the man piled out of the still-rocking car. 'He's not dead!' he snapped. 'Get him to hospital quick. Looks like a fractured skull.'

The sergeant knelt quickly, and grunted when Tern's words were confirmed. 'Did you see what happened?' he demanded. 'I thought I saw a youth or something jump from that window up there. The light was bad, though.'

'No youth!' snarled Tern almost savagely. 'It was more like a monster, a cross between a mechanical man and a jack-in-the-box. Didn't you see the size of its head, and the way it moved? For God's sake, man, get cracking!'

Two more cars and three running constables arrived on the scene. Tern, against his will, was bundled into one of the cars and driven off at high speed. The rest of the party went to work on entering the laboratory block. Before he left, Tern got a hearing from the sergeant.

'Someone's in there hurt,' he said. 'Brooking, if I'm not mistaken! And you'll probably find a body, too. If you do, it'll belong to Gregory Conrad. Brooking's got blood on his hands and his white jacket. There's a devil's brew for you.'

The sergeant had eyed him with a mixture of hostility, scepticism and interest. Whether he believed the yarn or not, Tern could not be sure. Dutch had been carefully removed by ambulance. All the smooth efficiency of the police machine was on the job.

At the station they questioned Tern,

checked his damaged leg, took a statement from him and told him to consider himself lucky he wasn't under arrest. 'You'd better stay here for the rest of the night,' he was told.

'But I have to get my story in!' he protested. 'I work for a living, damn it!'

'So do we, Tern. Wait till we get leave to release you. And don't start talking about unlawful arrest!'

'What is this, then — a convalescent home, or what?'

The station sergeant grinned, offering a cigarette. 'You can call it that if you like,' he replied. 'For your own good, that's all. This story of yours about the figure that jumped from Brooking's place may be true. On the other hand, you may have been mistaken. Whatever hit the inspector did a wonderful job. No boy or youth could have hit so hard.'

Tern blinked. 'You mean you don't believe me? But the sergeant in the car saw it too!'

'He only thinks he saw something jump. You're the one who gave a description, Tern. We wouldn't want anything to happen to you, that's all.'

Tern grunted. His leg was stiff but not impossible to move. He was deciding whether to try to make a break for it when the desk phone jangled. The sergeant picked it up. When he had finished a brief and singularly one-sided conversation with the unseen caller, he glanced at Tern, nodded to the instrument and said goodbye. Then he eyed Tern sternly and folded his hands together.

'Someone's lying,' he murmured slowly. 'There was no blood, no body, no Brooking in the lab. They combed the entire place. Nothing of an incriminating nature to be found. Are you sure you saw what you say you saw through that window before you fell? Or were you dreaming?'

Tern made a disgusted noise. 'So I'm a liar!' he snapped. 'I tell you again, and I'll go on repeating it, that when I saw Brooking last he had blood on his hands and was doing something that simply must have been very unethical. If you don't believe me, you can go and chase yourselves. The fact that poor old Dutch was of the same opinion doesn't carry any weight, I suppose?' He lurched to his feet and made for the door of the office. 'Anyhow I'm going now, whether you like it or not. And you can't hold me without a charge, which you haven't got!'

The sergeant wore a sad, resigned expression as Tern left the office.

Jerry Tern limped painfully out into the grey of a foggy dawn. He still had to write up a story — and persuade his editor it was a true one. At any rate, there was more solid evidence to back it this time, even if no one believed his theory that Gregory Conrad had been murdered and disposed of by the now-missing scientist.

A cruising taxi came by. He thought about the woman he had met in the night. He thought about the whole incredible set-up and wondered if he wasn't really dreaming as the police sergeant had seemed to think. But he knew he was sane enough about it. There was some queer happening to account for, and a very queer being on the loose, something with an enormous head and a body like a boy's, only it wasn't a proper human body.

At his office he was greeted sceptically, with little sympathy for his injured leg. And when he had hammered out the story, the sub was even more sceptical, insisting that a splash featuring the murderous attack on a police inspector by something that was half-human, half-robot would not be printed without considerably more to go on. He went to the trouble of impressing on Tern that the paper was famous for its truthfulness and lack of sensationalism. Tern remained unimpressed, grew somewhat angry, and said he would find another rag where initiative was appreciated. The atmosphere was rapidly becoming heated when he limped through the outer office on his way to unemployment. Not that Tern worried very much.

He had almost reached the door when someone started to speak on a phone, getting a story. The incredulous excitement in the man's voice halted Tern against his will. He stopped and moved across to the desk, glancing down at the scribbled shorthand as the reporter took it down. Then he slammed the phone back and stared up at Tern.

'D'you get that, Jerry?' he demanded. 'If this is true, there's a cannibal loose! My God, it doesn't seem possible, but Jack isn't usually wrong.'

Tern seized the pad as others crowded round, gathering because of the evident excitement.

A young woman had been brutally murdered, her skull crushed like an eggshell. But that was not the worst of it. The body, according to the report, had been torn and horribly mutilated as if some creature had set on it after death with savage fangs.

Tern was still piecing the news together when the story went through to the editor. The more he gathered, the less he liked the sound of it. The murder had taken place less than an hour ago. And someone had caught a glimpse of a strange figure moving swiftly away from the scene of the killing. The figure had been small, very quick-moving, and had a large head. The witness, a road-sweeper, said the figure appeared to be blue in colour, and quite bald, a freak.

'It's the same thing that battered Dutch,' Tern said. 'I saw it myself, damn it! No one will believe me, but this is the beginning of a reign of terror!'

One of the men rubbed his face with the flat of his hand. They were silent for a space.

'The Blue Peril,' suggested someone else. 'Headline it, Joe!'

Tern looked again at the details of the story. Then he left the office in a hurry, ignoring the plea of the sub to take his job back and stick on the case. The location of the murder had not registered in his mind at first, but now he realised with a terrible sinking feeling that the Blue Peril had struck within a few yards of Vivienne Conrad's home. The chain of circumstance that had so far linked her to Brooking and the things that Brooking did spurred Tern on with icicles of deep-rooted fear.

The fog had come down more thickly when he secured a taxi and rumbled through the grey-yellow gloom. He found his anxiety growing with every slow-crawling yard of progress, but the fog was a hindrance.

4

The Cellar

There was still a small crowd gathered on the pavement when Tern arrived. He caught sight of three helmeted heads and a group of staring, goggling people, early workers pausing on their way, perhaps not even knowing what it was all about. The lights in the house windows were dim and yellow in the fog. Several doors were open.

Tern elbowed his way through the crowd, showing his card to one of the policemen. They were not interested; several other newspaper men had already been, it appeared. There was nothing to see. The body had been found on the cold damp pavement just about where they were standing. No, it had not been identified yet.

Tern wormed his way quickly to the house where Vivienne lived. It was frighteningly close to the murder scene. His heart was thumping as he ran up the steps and thumbed the bell-push. As the seconds ticked by, they stretched out to eternity in his strained imagination. Then the door opened and the pale foggy light fell on Vivienne's face.

For an instant Tern held his breath, then he seized her hands and gripped them tightly. 'Thank heaven you're all right!' he muttered awkwardly. 'I was so afraid . . . '

She swallowed. 'Come in,' she said. 'You're not the only one to be scared.' At the sight of him, she exhibited genuine signs of relief and pleasure.

He stepped in and stood while she closed the door on the fog of the morning. She was still wearing a dressing gown over pyjamas, with small blue mules on her feet. *Blue,* he thought . . .

The light was on in a room towards the back of the house. He followed her down the hallway.

'Coffee?' she said. 'Have you had your breakfast yet?'

He shook his head. 'No time,' he

admitted. 'Quite a lot has happened since we parted.' While he told her about Happy Dutch and the events of the night, she was busy with a frying pan on the gas stove. A certain sense of camaraderie had sprung up between them now, removing all the awkwardness there might so easily have been.

'It was frightful,' she said when he had finished. 'I heard a terrible cry while I was still asleep. It woke me up. When I looked out of the window I saw *something* bending over what must have been the body not far away. The light was too bad to see anything clearly, of course, and the fog didn't help either.' She paused. 'If I'd known it was the thing that you saw jump from Brooking's laboratory, I'd have had a fit!'

Tern was worried and not a little puzzled. Why, he asked himself, had the Blue Peril come to this particular neighbourhood from the lab? Was it a mere coincidence, or had something else guided it — something connected with Conrad that led it to where his sister lived? There was fear in the thought, for if it had substance it might come again. Unless, of course, the police effected a capture. But somehow when Tern remembered that incredible speed of which the creature was capable, he began to wonder whether they would catch it so simply.

They breakfasted, discussing the strange events. 'What are you going to do now that you're out of a job?' Vivienne asked quietly.

Tern eyed her ruefully. Then the old grin spread across his face. 'Take a holiday,' he said. 'A useful break in which I might even dig up something really worthwhile.'

She frowned. 'About my brother, you mean?'

He nodded wordlessly.

'Where will you start? I — I'd like to help, if you'll have me.'

He pondered, although he already knew the result. 'Now that Brooking has disappeared, I should very much like to make a thorough search of his lab,' he said. 'The police will be nosing around, naturally, but we might slip past them. You see, Vivienne, I'm certain he didn't leave that building between the time I heard a scream and the moment the police arrived and surrounded the place. Either he's still inside it, or he has a bolt hole we don't know about. There's also the problem of what became of your brother. It's never been settled — not to my satisfaction, anyway.'

She pushed back the hair from her forehead and smiled. 'When do we start, Jerry? You're a pretty nice person, aren't you?'

He grinned. 'Shall we do the washing up now?'

'Leave it,' she said. 'I'll go and dress. Be with you in ten minutes dead.'

Tern was thoughtful as he piled the plates in the sink and sluiced them clean. He wondered if he was wise in bringing Vivienne into the picture; but at least if he took her into partnership, he would know more or less where she was all the time. And with a thing like the Blue Peril floating around loose, it would be better for his peace of mind.

She was wearing a smartly cut black costume when she showed up again. Her head was bare, but she carried a small black hat in one hand and a bag in the other. Side by side they headed for the front door. 'This fog will wreck my hair,' she complained.

He shot her an appreciative sidelong glance. Nothing could wreck her hair, he thought. Aloud he said: 'Put your hat on.'

A taxi dropped them in the neighbourhood of the laboratory. Tern's plan of action was vague; and the fog, denser than ever now, was more help than hindrance. Leaving the taxi, they bought an early paper. It contained a garbled version of the murder and mention, too, of the attack on Inspector Dutch, who was stated to be still unconscious. There were, however, wild rumours and even wilder descriptions of the assailant. The British public at its breakfast tables was expected to believe that some fantastic creature with the strength of a Goliath and a stature ranging from that of a pigmy to a thing of enormous proportions was at large in the metropolis.

Tern's face was grim as he and Vivienne read the news by the light of a street lamp that struggled weakly through the pall of fog. 'In this murk, if the brute is still around it won't find much difficulty in staying hidden,' he grunted. 'Come on, we've got to get inside that block somehow or other. I'll swear there's something more to be learnt.'

A policeman stood on guard outside the front entrance. There was a second on duty at the yard gate from the alley behind. Tern and Vivienne circled the entire block in silence. 'I think we can get in,' Tern said quietly. 'Did you see that fire escape leading up to the roof of the office two doors down from the lab?'

She nodded. 'Over the roof-tops?'

He took her arm and pressed it firmly. 'Watch your nylons. Let's have a try!'

It was considerably simpler than either of them had expected. The fog swirled round them as they gained the first roof. Tern was delighted to see that the roofs were flat, with high stone parapets all round them. 'This way,' he said. He gripped her arm more tightly. A low stone wall separated the buildings in the block, leaving each with a roof like a school playground, except that in the centre of each was a big skylight giving access to the top storey.

A brief tussle with the one above the laboratory block was enough. The thing had not been opened for years in all probability, and the hinges rasped alarmingly. But there were no indications that Brooking might have left the building by this route.

He lowered himself through, hanging by his hands for an instant before letting go. The drop was short but jarred his leg into pain. He cursed silently and listened, then looked up at where Vivienne stood on the edge of the open trap. A moment later she slid over and he caught her knees, steadying her. Then she was on the floor, breathing rather quickly and peering down the corridor in which they found themselves. The place was deathly quiet. Faint daylight permeated the corridor at its far end, but the area was dusty and plainly not in regular use.

Walking on tiptoe, they reached a bare uncarpeted stair. 'This is the third floor we're on,' Tern whispered. 'The next one down is where I watched Brooking early this morning.' He used his flashlight, searching with it; then they started down.

Only when they had been through the entire premises from top to bottom, and finally returned disappointed to the upper laboratory, did good fortune smile on them.

'The police are right,' Tern grunted. 'There isn't anything incriminating here. And yet . . . ' He gestured resignedly. 'I'm positive my eyes didn't deceive me!'

Vivienne was wandering round the room, examining things. Suddenly she stiffened and turned towards him. 'Come here!' she breathed. 'You were right, Jerry!'

He was at her side in a moment. 'What is it?'

She had dropped to her knees and was pointing to the floor in front of the wall opposite the window from which he had come to grief. 'That mark,' she whispered. 'Isn't it a tiny smear of blood on the floor?'

He examined it more closely, using the flashlight again. Then he turned the light upwards. There was a row of shelves immediately over the spot, and an even closer examination revealed the fact that the entire block of shelves appeared to be a separate structure from the ones flanking it on each side. Excitement grew within him, for it was obvious that the small smear of blood did not end at the wall, but extended beneath the bottom board of the shelving block.

Without voicing his hopes he went to work, and a few moments later the shelves swung outwards en bloc, to reveal a dark recess in which the thin steel ropes of a lift were visible.

Tern whistled softly. 'Now we're getting somewhere!' he murmured. 'So this is the way friend Brooking ducked out. Do you know what I think actually happened?'

'That blood smear ... ' Vivienne muttered. 'Something was dragged over the edge and put in the lift cage. But what?'

'Brooking was attacked by the monster. That was the scream I heard. He was knocked for six, and the monster made for the front of the building, jumping from the window. Before the police could get around to searching the place, Brooking had come to, dumped anything incriminating in the lift, and then added himself to the load. This thing is frequently used; you can tell by the oil on the slides.'

'Are we going to use it?' Vivienne's eyes were wide and troubled.

'If you're game!'

'Of course I am!'

He hauled on the rope, drawing up the cage. The shaft was deep, and it was a good five minutes before the cage appeared in the opening. Vivienne held her breath as it came into view, but it was empty. There were, however, several tell-tale marks on the wooden planks of the floor.

'You're sure you wouldn't rather stay up here?' Tern said.

Vivienne shook her head. 'You're not going to leave me out of this,' she insisted. 'Let's get it over with.'

They crowded into the cage; there was not a great deal of room. Inside was a control lever, a brake acting on the ropes. The descent seemed endless, but at last a red light came to life and Tern used the lever, slowing the cage. A moment later it jerked to a halt, and they found themselves staring out into darkness so intense that for a second or two they remained where they were.

The beam of the flashlight showed a bare concrete room like a cellar, but apparently intended only for the bottom end of the lift run. Opening off it was a dark passage.

'Are you feeling brave?' Tern whispered as they stepped from the lift and peered about. 'That's the only way, through there.'

Vivienne's hand came groping for his as he spoke. Then they were moving forward together, heading down the passage with the blob of light from the torch dancing ahead. Even to Tern there was something strangely macabre in the journey. He thought his companion must be scared stiff, but she never faltered.

'There's a door in front,' she breathed nervously.

It was true: a steel door barred their way some twenty yards from where they had entered the passageway. Tern came to a halt, listening, his head to one side and his fingers hard on Vivienne's wrist. No sound broke the stillness. He let go of her and reached for the doorknob, turning it slowly and carefully, conscious of being unarmed for the first time since beginning this crazy search for Brooking.

With the door open just far enough to peer through the gap, he flashed his torch round the walls of a large low-roofed cellar. Somewhat to his surprise, the place was furnished sparsely, and there were signs that it had recently been used. Tern stepped in through the doorway with Vivienne close on his heels.

Almost instantly an electric light bulb flared into life from the ceiling, and a harsh voice ordered them to stand still. At the same time the steel door slammed shut behind Vivienne. Tern spun round as if stung, to find himself looking into the face of Brooking; the man had been concealed behind the door when it opened. There was a short-nosed automatic in his hand, and from the look in his eyes there appeared to be every chance of his using it with little compunction.

Vivienne stifled a gasp and grabbed at Tern's arm. Tern became as rigid as an iron girder, his eyes narrowed grimly, all the innate humour swept from his face.

'Hello, Brooking,' he said very softly. 'I didn't expect to find you down here.'

Brooking's lips twisted maliciously. It might have been a smile; but whatever the expression, it was ugly. 'What *did* you expect to find for your prying?' he asked.

Tern considered. 'Conrad, perhaps . . . Who knows? Why the gun, anyway? It hardly makes for a civil atmosphere among friends, if I may say so.'

'I am careful in my choice of friends,' Brooking murmured. 'This young woman's brother has already injured my faith in the human race — or perhaps you did not hear about his duplicity, Miss Conrad?'

'She knows!' grated Tern. He felt the chair seat behind him and sat down cautiously. 'Where is he now?'

'Wherever people like him go when they die — if a man dies when a part of

66

his body is still living, of course. It is a question singularly difficult to answer at this stage in scientific advancement. However, it is of no importance from your point of view.' He moved his gun slightly from side to side, keeping them covered in turn, his eyes never wavering, though there was a wild gleam of incipient insanity in their glitter.

Tern shot an anxious glance at Vivienne. He was sorry he had ever suggested bringing her into this, but recriminations were useless. They were both up against it, and a man of Brooking's calibre was no mean adversary — especially when he was obviously more than half-crazy.

'You killed my brother!' Vivienne's voice was tense in the quiet hiatus. 'Why couldn't you say so outright?'

Brooking came closer to them now, crouching forward a little, his head thrust out. 'I could say a lot of things outright, my dear!' he whispered dangerously. 'I could tell you straightaway that you will not leave here alive. But I prefer to let it sink in slowly so that you may both savour the niceties of the situation to the full.'

Tern shifted a little, easing himself on the chair. His muscles were tautening up now. Before long there would have to be some slick work if this present scene was not to end in bloodshed. For the moment, though, Brooking would talk; and all the time he talked he would not be shooting.

'Did you create that monster that jumped through a window in the night?' Tern demanded. 'I know you were doing something, because I saw a little of what was going on. Then you let out a scream, and a moment or two afterwards something jumped into the street below. A thing like a boy, with a head several times the size of a normal man's.'

Brooking showed interest. 'You saw it?' he cried in a tone of excitement. 'What was it doing? How did it move? You must tell me instantly!' His hand was shaking unsteadily, and he concentrated all his attention on Tern.

'Yes, Brooking, I saw it. I saw it nearly kill Inspector Dutch, then disappear. It's at large in the city now. A few hours ago it murdered a woman, mutilating the body with its teeth. People are saying it meant to eat her, but must have been disturbed.'

Brooking paled perceptibly. 'It has *killed*?' he said in an awed whisper. 'But — I don't understand! It had no cause to murder, surely?'

Tern shrugged. 'I should say you're the best one to answer that,' he retorted. 'Tell us about it. Conrad comes into it somewhere, doesn't he? You've got us where you want us, so it doesn't matter what you tell us now.' He tried to sound defiant, but all the time was watching Brooking like a hawk watches a mouse before pouncing.

Brooking smiled and glanced at Vivienne, who was as white as a sheet. Tern was sorry he had had to mention her brother, but time was a valuable commodity right now; and if only Brooking would keep on talking, a chance to escape might present itself.

'Conrad does come into the picture, as you say,' murmured the scientist. 'More into it than you imagine!' He broke off and gave a dry chuckle, but his vigilance in no way relaxed. This was the cunning, the craftiness of a madman.

'I brought life and movement to an inanimate structure,' he went on. His voice was pitched lower now, tense with suppressed excitement. 'I actually fashioned with my own hands a human figure, partially using synthetic materials and partially human tissue for essential organs. The entire undertaking was revolutionary, a miracle of modern science! I have achieved what no other man has ever attempted in the past! And I have succeeded, I tell you!' He leant forward, his eyes gleaming madly, the gun in his hand shaking.

Tern stared back bleakly. 'You've succeeded in doing something for which a hundred people may pay with their lives,' he said. 'A woman had to die in the first place to satisfy your need for human tissue. Conrad objected. In the end you were forced to kill him as well. What happened, Brooking? Did you need some more living tissue?'

Brooking chuckled hideously. 'What I

needed at that late stage in development was a brain!' he said quietly. 'A human brain, do you understand? That was what I needed, and that was what I got.' He sneered as Vivienne suddenly covered her face with her hands, sobbing uncontrollably. 'You have no courage to face the facts,' he added callously. 'For me it was essential to do what I did. Progress will always be served; it *must* be served! Your worthless brother did more useful service in death than he ever did during his life. His brain is now an active part of highly stimulated growth in the skull of an artificial being; a being, moreover, which is an entirely separate entity, needing no guidance or direction from me, its creator. It can stand on its own feet.'

'It can kill and slaughter and mutilate and wreak havoc among innocent people!' snapped Tern. 'But I suppose that doesn't worry you! Aren't you afraid of it yourself?'

Brooking hesitated for a split second, which gave them an inkling of the latent fear in his heart. 'Of course I'm not afraid of it!' he snarled. 'I'm hiding down here

71

because the police would pester me with questions if they had a chance.'

Tern nodded thoughtfully. 'They certainly would,' he agreed. 'They don't believe what you told them about Conrad now; they believe you murdered him. You'll have to stay in hiding a darned long time to slip out of this mess!'

Brooking smiled again. 'A pleasure which you will unfortunately not be in a position to share with me,' he said. 'I regret the necessity, but am compelled to kill you both. You are dangerous witnesses, and quite apart from that there is little accommodation down here for more than one person.'

Tern sighed resignedly. 'That's a pity, Brooking,' he murmured with a shake of his head. 'I might have been able to give you one or two hints on how to make your escape more complete — without the tedious waiting enforced on you at the moment. We might even make a deal if you're interested. There are worse things than being in the same country as this Blue Peril you've brought to life!'

Brooking hesitated, eyeing him with a

mixture of tension and plain suspicion. There was interest there, fear of the future, the spark of hope. He touched his tongue to his lips, then suddenly squared his shoulders. 'No!' he said. 'You'll have to die, and the sooner the better. Conrad's body is already disposed of; yours will follow.

And behind him the door was opening . . .

5

Hostages of Terror

It was a moment — a frozen second when time seemed to come to a standstill completely — that Tern was never to forget or look back on without an involuntary shudder at the memory of it.

Brooking's finger was tightening on the trigger of the automatic, its barrel aimed directly at Vivienne. Tern bunched himself for a last desperate leap, ready to take the shot and so save her, not giving death a thought as the clock became momentarily stationary.

And all the while, the door was opening inch by inch. Not until Brooking's intention was plain did either of the other two notice the movement, so intent were they on their captor. It was Vivienne who first caught a glimpse of the blue shadowy thing that was coming in. Heedless of the threatening gun, she screamed and pointed.

At the same time Brooking hesitated, half-turning his head. Tern seized his chance and hurled himself forward, aware that in a moment the Blue Peril itself would be with them. His shoulder crashed against Brooking. Before the scientist could fire again or regain his balance, he had gone backwards straight for the door, staggering as he went, to be seized and held by the monstrous apparition now standing in full view on the threshold.

The scientist was powerless in its steely grip, but he made a desperate attempt to turn round and bring his gun to bear on his captor. The creature itself seemed to sense this danger, releasing one hand and clenching its fist. It used it as a child might, hammering downwards on Brooking's head. There was a dull thud and the scientist collapsed in a motionless sprawl on the ground. The Blue Peril picked up the automatic.

Tern seemed to have lost the use of his muscles entirely, so paralysed was he by the sight of this incredible being. He could only stare aghast at the soulless eyes; the hideous face with its open nostrils and cold slit mouth; the enormous ungainly head and small plastic arms and legs.

Then it spoke for the first time. If anything, the sound of its voice was even more terrifying than its form.

'I strike fear into your hearts because I am ugly,' it said. There was a sneering, half-human, half-mechanical cadence in the words, a horrifying intonation that made Tern catch his breath. Suddenly he was aware of Vivienne again. She gave a choking little sob, and her weight against him was dead and motionless.

'She has fainted,' said the thing. 'Fear can strike as deadly as a bullet, Tern. Lift her up and comfort her.'

Tern gaped at it, amazement growing up inside him alongside involuntary terror. It had called him by name! And how could it know about people fainting? An awful notion that this creature of Brooking's creation was superhuman came to his mind. He knew it could not be possible, yet how else was he to explain its unexpected knowledge?

Then he slid an arm round Vivienne and raised her limp form from beside him. She had slithered half out of her chair into which she had sunk but a moment before. Her eyes were closed and her face was bloodless. Tern was suddenly filled an anxiety that had nothing to do with the presence of the Blue Peril. He knew in a flash that this woman was important to him; that her happiness was as much his own as the hair on his head. And there was little of happiness in his life at the moment.

Still supporting her, he looked again at the thing. It had moved soundlessly nearer, ignoring Brooking completely. 'She will be all right,' it said in the same thin, piping voice. 'You need not be afraid for her, Tern. Brooking would have killed you both if I had not arrived.'

Tern licked his lips nervously. His heart was making so much commotion in his chest that he thought it must be audible. 'What — what are you?' he gasped. 'You nearly killed a policeman, a friend of mine. Later you savaged a woman. Have you no human decency, whatever you are?'

It considered carefully — or appeared to — before answering. Then: 'If human decency is exemplified by the traits of Brooking, I would rather be without it. To build me and bring me to life, that man took the lives of two people. Life does not matter to me, but now that I have it I shall keep it for various reasons, revenge being chief among them. To me, all mankind is an enemy, and I am powerful enough to do considerable damage.'

Tern listened, alert for some point of weakness. There was none. 'How did you know my name?' he asked.

The creature made a grimace that might well have been a grin of sardonic amusement. 'I had an idea that would puzzle you,' it replied. 'You will discover in time that there is little I do not know, if I choose to concentrate hard enough on anything for a short while. That is my strength, and therein lies my ability to wage a war on the human race.'

'You're mad!' gasped Tern.

'By what standards? Human degrees of madness are of no consequence in my case. Suppose I was captured and tried by your courts? I don't happen to be a human being in the accepted sense of the word. That would fox them, would it not?' The thing broke off and chuckled quietly.

'You'll never be brought to justice that way,' said Tern. 'You'll be hunted like a wild animal — with rifles!'

'In which case it is even more fortunate for me that you discovered this hide-out. You and Vivienne will be useful, Tern. Especially Vivienne . . . '

Tern licked his lips, his eyes darting this way and that. There was no escape from here, he knew that, and his heart sank. 'Why do you say so?' he demanded.

'Because a hunted creature needs company and someone else to act as a link with the rest of the world. You two will serve that purpose admirably.' The slit mouth twisted in a semblance of a smile as Tern glanced anxiously at Vivienne. 'No,' it went on, 'you needn't be afraid for her sake. If it suits me I shall kill you both; you won't have to worry on other counts. Remember that I'm not wholly human.'

Vivienne stirred beside him, returning to her senses. He was glad she had not been listening to most of the conversation. Her eyes were wide with horror as she saw the monster again. Tern slid an arm round her shoulders. 'It means us no harm,' he whispered. 'We're . . . hostages of a kind, I fancy.'

'You put the position clearly, Tern,' he was told. 'And now shall we discuss the immediate future?'

Tern shrugged, trying not to appear disturbed. 'What did you have in mind?'

'The question of moving from here to a more mobile place of concealment. Concrete walls, I find, have a cramping effect on me.' It paused and stared round the cellar.

'You'll find a grave more cramping still!' snapped Tern. Without the slightest warning he lunged forward, past Vivienne to grapple with the man-made being.

He might as well have hurled himself at a brick wall. The first thing he knew was an odd effect that his feet had left the ground, and he was floating backwards at tremendous speed. Then he landed with a crash on the ground, all the breath knocked from his body. And the monster was standing over him, grinning wickedly, the gun in its hand covering Vivienne.

'It is fortunate that I need you alive,' it said flatly. 'Otherwise I should have hit you harder. Now get up, and for her sake don't try that kind of thing again. You've had your warning, Tern; take it to heart!'

Tern crawled to his feet. His chest felt as if most of the bones were cracked, and he was staggered by the speed of the blow he had received. It had been so swift that quite literally he never saw it coming. This creature, he decided ruefully, was a potent enemy — even without a gun.

Vivienne, after a single yelp of dismay, had run to his aid, kneeling beside him before he rose. For some reason or other he felt a surge of pleasure at her nearness, and that in spite of the desperate situation they were in.

The Blue Peril stepped back beyond the prostrate form of Brooking. The scientist was still unconscious, proof of the monster's strength. 'You are ready to behave like a rational being?' it demanded of Tern.

Tern dusted his clothes and glared back belligerently.

'That will depend on what you mean!' he growled. 'Personally I think you'll end up dead before long, but that'll be your affair. What do you want of us?'

The being eyed him coldly for a moment. 'There will be times when I shall find it advisable to remain in hiding,' it replied. 'On such occasions some link with outside events and personalities will be useful. That is where you come into the picture, Tern. And that, if I may say so, is where Vivienne Conrad will prove her worth as well. She will be my safeguard at times when you are away from us.'

The idea slowly dawned on Tern that they were to be kept as prisoners by the thing, yet prisoners with a certain amount of freedom, the safety of one depending on the good behaviour of the other. There was more than human cunning in the scheme; it was devilish, he thought. But just at the moment the Blue Peril definitely had the upper hand.

'You're clever,' he said aloud. 'Don't be

overly confident, though. We have a human adage about there being many a slip. You wouldn't know about that; or would you?'

'I know about it, Tern, don't worry yourself. And now for action! We are leaving here, and the life of this woman rests entirely in your own hands. Try to trick me, or call attention to what is going on, and she will die at once. If you remember that, everything will be all right; forget it and I need not impress on you the consequences. Are you ready?'

Tern looked round the room. 'Which way?' he asked. 'If you go back the way we came, you're certain to run into the police. That wouldn't do you much good — us either.'

The being chuckled. Tern thought it was the most horrible sound he had ever heard in his life; he grew to dread it and hate it with the passing seconds.

'You know very little of Brooking's past activities,' the monster said slowly. 'There is another escape route from here. Why do you think he built this cellar if it was only a dead end? How do you think he disposed of the bodies if there was nowhere to take them once he was down here? You are a bigger fool than I thought. However, there is no doubt there will be times when you may come in useful.'

Vivienne clung to Tern's arm nervously. She averted her eyes from the monster whenever it looked in her direction, but it made no move to approach her more closely. Then it gestured to the wall behind Tern. 'Brooking has always been something of a craftsman when it comes to manufacturing gadgets, you know. If you examine the concrete very closely, you will observe a hairline crack in the structure. It forms a second exit, and by devious means brings one to . . . But you shall see in a few minutes, for that is the route we shall take.'

Vivienne cringed away as the being advanced towards them. Tern stood aside, curious now, some of his instinctive fear leaving him. How this creature knew so much was something he had not discovered; something he would like to know. But for now it must wait; there were more vital issues at stake.

The Blue Peril, always managing to keep one eye on Tern and Vivienne, pressed a concealed button in the wall. In a moment the section surrounded by that unnoticed hairline crack quivered and opened inwards, revealing a dark passage-way wide enough for two persons to walk abreast.

'You will walk ahead,' said the being. 'And remember that I have this weapon and know how to use it. It will be Vivienne who suffers first.'

'You don't have to rub it in!' snapped Tern. He took Vivienne's arm and started into the gloomy tunnel. After a few yards — just when he was considering if the darkness would cover a dash — a whole string of electric bulbs came to life in the shallow arch of the roof. The monster did not seem to miss much, he thought wryly. In fact there was little it failed to discover or utilise. He wondered uneasily if it was capable of reading their thoughts.

The passageway went on and on for what seemed like miles. Here and there it turned abruptly. Every turn was a right angle, but Tern noticed that most of them cancelled out so that progress was always away from the beginning of the tunnel.

The creature at their backs made little or no noise, but whenever Tern glanced over his shoulder it was never very far in the rear. At the end of each straight length of tunnel, it switched off the preceding lights and switched on the next section of illumination. And there was no chance of their being followed, Tern realised, because the creature had shut the irregularly shaped door to this underground warren.

'You have not much further to walk,' came its voice from behind them. 'Another hundred yards or so.'

'Where the devil does this come out?' demanded Tern in an irritable tone.

'You will see soon. For the moment, contain your impatience and just keep moving.'

Tern pressed Vivienne's arm reassuringly, trying to tell her that their chance would come before long; that a moment would arrive when a desperate bid would be rewarded by freedom. She seemed to understand, shooting him a grateful glance in which the hint of a wan smile showed up at the back of her eyes.

Then the tunnel ended and they stopped of their own accord. To their ears came the sullen splash of water; and the thick smell of the Thames — tidal mud, smoke and fog all mixed — touched their nostrils. Through cracks in a rough wooden door they glimpsed light as the Blue Peril switched off the last of the electric circuits.

'Open the door, Tern!' it ordered curtly. 'No tricks, either!'

Tern felt over the planking for a handle, found it and gave it a twist. There was a creaking sound and the door swung out-wards, spilling in the grey light from beyond. Tern peered out and found himself looking into what appeared to be a small warehouse, bare and empty and fronting on the river. But when he studied it more closely, he saw that an arm of water ran right inside from the river itself, and in the arm of black water lay a blue and cream motor cruiser, its bows pointing outwards.

'Move on,' said the monster quietly. 'This is where Gregory Conrad came with the first victim's body. It was near here that he was seen to dispose of it; hence he became a fugitive from justice, though innocent of murder. And it is to this place that Brooking brought Conrad's body when the vital portion of it had been extracted. This is the place from which Brooking himself could have escaped completely had he not been so big a fool.'

Tern and Vivienne stepped from the tunnel into the more open space of the building. To all intents and purposes the place was an innocent private boat-house, though rather a large one. Tern stared at the cruiser. That it was Brooking's, he had no doubt; and when a moment later the Blue Peril urged them towards it, the idea was confirmed.

'Brooking kept this for emergencies,' said the monster. 'The boat-house is well known to the river police, and Brooking himself owns the premises. He frequently uses the boat, or did until recently. Naturally, no one is aware of the way it was used. Brooking has always been a careful person.'

Tern glanced at it angrily. 'What do you expect us to do now?' he inquired. 'Go for a trip on the Thames?'

'Not just at the moment; that will undoubtedly come later on when I am ready to establish a headquarters some-where. For now you will go aboard the cruiser.'

Tern, still gripping Vivienne's arm, tried to decide if an attack on the creature would be successful. In the end he reached the conclusion that the risk to Vivienne was too great, so shelved the notion. Instead he piloted her towards the stern of the vessel and stepped aboard, glancing out through the fog-shrouded front of the building. There was no sign of assistance in that direction. The fog clamped down so thickly that he could see no more than a yard or two of sullenly rippling water beyond the entrance. The only feature of the position that gave him some hope was that according to the Blue Peril, the police were familiar with Brooking's ownership of the place. A time would come when they would search it, connecting the presence of a boat with some possible plan for escape.

The cruiser was large, a powerful sea and estuary craft. Under the prompting of their captor, the two of them crossed the companionway and stood in the roomy saloon.

'It is obviously necessary for me to remain concealed,' said the monster. 'Quite plainly, too, it is necessary that I should eat. The same goes for you, of course. But there is no food on board this vessel, and that is one reason why I am enlisting you.'

Tern caught his breath, remembering a report that the body of the murdered woman near Vivienne's home had been torn as if by savage fangs. The monster seemed to read his thoughts, for it smiled hideously and shook its head.

'You need not be afraid that I shall eat Vivienne,' it said. 'Not unless I am forced to, that is . . . I have a certain regard for her over all other humans, perhaps because the tissue of which my brain is composed once belonged to her brother, Gregory. However, that is not the point. The immediate need is for you, Tern, to go and get supplies for the three of us.'

Tern coloured angrily. 'I'll see you in hell before doing that!' he snapped.

'You mean you'll condemn Vivienne to death. That is what refusal would amount to. No, you will walk out of here quite naturally and bring back some food. If you fail to return — or, worse still, if you bring anyone back with you — Vivienne will die. No action on your part could save her, and you have already tasted some of the speed with which I can move when I have to. Are you willing to take the risk? I promise you that nothing will happen to Vivienne while you are away, but heaven help her if you try to double-cross me. Even if I begin to suspect such a thing, I shall act at once.'

Vivienne's eyes were eloquent of despair and fear, but Tern knew he was faced by a problem defying a solution except by doing as he was told. There was nothing else for it. 'What is it you need?' he demanded reluctantly. 'And how can I be sure that you'll keep your side of the bargain?'

The monster smiled slightly. 'I shall

keep it because it suits me to,' it said. 'As to what we need, a few supplies to go on with will be sufficient; say enough for a couple of days on our own. My immediate plan is to run downriver out of the search area. Just to make life more comfortable, you understand?'

'I'll be back in half an hour,' said Tern. He looked at Vivienne. 'Honestly,' he added, 'we shall have to trust it, my dear. I don't think you'll come to any harm, and I won't be long.'

The monster wagged its enormous head. 'She will be all right,' it said. 'Remember that for now she is my hostage, nothing worse than that. If she were to die without need, my hold on you would vanish, and I may need you even more at some later date. Are we quite clear on that?'

Tern sighed. 'Very well.'

'There is a normal outside door to the building over there, Tern. Use it and you will find yourself in a street. Don't forget to come back.'

6

Fog on the River

Tern, his mind in a whirl of troubled thoughts, wasted no time once he had located the exit door and reached the street. It was little more than a mean alleyway between warehouses on one side and the boat-house on the other, but presently it opened into a busier thoroughfare in which the gloom of the fog was shot by pale yellow blobs of light from street lamps. It was hard to believe, he reflected, that the time was now almost eleven o'clock on an autumn morning.

From the unseen river came the eerie, rather mournful hoot of a ship's siren as the vessel felt its way downstream. In the distance, too, car horns were strident, muffled by the fog. Some heavily laden vehicle rumbled past on the street only a few yards away from him, its side-lamps liverish eyes in the dense grey moisture.

He took careful note of where he was, waiting till he could be sure of finding his way back. There was no hope in his mind of turning the tables on the monster at this stage, and his one intention was to get the necessary stores and then hurry back to Vivienne.

A dark figure loomed up in front of him, grunting as it almost collided with him. Tern sidestepped and continued. Presently a patch of glowing illumination heralded a shop. He heaved a sigh of relief as he recognised a food store and went in, closing the door behind him. The place was small and none too clean, but provided the simple things he must take.

He was halfway back to the alleyway entrance when a sound he dreaded came to his ears. From somewhere in his rear came the shrill blast of a police whistle, followed almost immediately by the thud of running footsteps, vague shouts and the grinding of hurriedly meshed gears as a truck started up.

The last thing Tern wanted was to be embroiled in a police hunt of any kind, whether it had anything to do with the monster or not. Fear gripped his heart when he thought of what the creature might do to Vivienne at the sound of a police whistle. He began to run, dodging down the narrow pavement, hugging his bag of supplies to his chest as he ran. The strain made his leg ache damnably. Then someone crashed into him from the opposite direction. He cursed and jumped clear, but the whistles were being reinforced in the background, and the man who had collided with him suddenly took it into his head that this was the fugitive.

With commendable speed and disregard for danger, the man, who seemed very large to Tern, grabbed him tightly and started to yell at the top of his voice. The thudding footsteps came closer. Several other people were closing in, also mistakenly believing that the wanted man had been caught.

Tern was desperate. He dropped his bag of provisions and lashed out like a madman, scoring a perfect hit on the man's exposed jaw. The man grunted, stopped yelling, and suddenly let go his grasp on Tern.

Tern was running again, running blindly through the fog, his main object being to escape from further embarrassment.

Instead, he ran straight into the arms of a singularly energetic figure who was poised for a rugger tackle only a few yards distant. The two became locked in each other's arms, twisting this way and that, panting for breath. But suddenly the other man stopped, thrusting his face close to Tern's.

'Jerry!' he gasped. 'What the hell's this? Are they after you?'

Tern gaped, muttered something under his breath and seized his adversary by the arm. 'Quick, Pete!' he snapped. 'Get moving, damn you! They'll be here in a second!' The noisy thud of footsteps was rapidly approaching now.

Peter Duval, a newspaper reporter like Tern, and an old friend, barely hesitated. 'I don't know what it's all about,' he grunted, 'but get a move on!'

Tern needed no further urging. With Duval at his side he scampered down the street, cursing his luck as he ran. His leg had stiffened up painfully, and had it not been for a helping hand from his colleague the pursuit would almost certainly have overtaken him. As it was, all sound of the pack died away before they had covered a quarter of a mile, the thin noise of the whistles seeming to go off on a tangent towards the river.

'You're safe now,' grunted Duval. He stopped and kept a hold on Tern's arm. 'Now,' he went on more grimly, 'tell me what's up.' He eyed Tern in the yellow gloom, trying to read his expression.

'Nothing's up, you clot!' Tern answered. 'I just didn't want to get involved in that chase, that's all. It wasn't anything to do with me. Who were they chasing, anyway?'

Duval seemed surprised. 'Fine newspaper man you are!' he said disgustedly. 'The police have been milling round that block, where the fellow Brooking lived and worked, for the past hour. Someone — they think it was Brooking — made a break and got clear, hence the fuss. He was thought to have ducked in this direction. I'm covering for my paper.'

'And I was working independently,'

said Tern. 'I had a hunch that didn't come off; the less said the better.' He was by now desperately anxious to shake off Duval and return to the cruiser, but his friend showed every sign of staying. Duval was a shrewd man with a nose for a mystery, and Tern knew quite well that at the moment he himself represented one.

'Let me in on this hunch,' said Duval firmly. 'Two are better than one when it comes to sorting something out. I might help, and we could share the story.'

'But it's nothing to do with Brooking and the murders!' Tern protested. 'This is something entirely separate. You stick to your own chore, pal.'

Duval grinned sardonically. 'You're a rotten liar, Jerry! Come on, out with it! Had an idea Brooking might try for that ship of his, I suppose? Well, maybe that was what he intended when he broke and ran from the lab. But he won't reach it. They've thrown a cordon on all streets giving access to the warehouse district. If he does try, it'll be too bad!'

Tern did not know whether to believe this information or not. But he was certainly a very worried man. What view would the Blue Peril take of all the noise of police activity? It would be the easiest thing imaginable for the thing to decide that he, Tern, was responsible. And Vivienne . . .

Glancing round in the murk, he suddenly struck out at Duval, landing a telling blow in his stomach. Then he was running as fast as his damaged leg would permit, sliding fast into the protective curtain of the fog.

Duval, recovering, shouted some abuse after him, but made no attempt to take up the chase. He must have thought Tern was crazy, or that he had guessed right about the boat-house stunt. Whichever way it was, Tern had a comparatively clear field, but wondered what had happened on the cruiser.

When he stopped running, it was to find to his dismay that he was hopelessly lost. The realisation brought renewed anxiety in its train. He halted and leant against a damp wall, getting his breath back and thinking fast. If Duval was right, Brooking had recovered his senses in the cellar and made a break by way of the building itself. The man was apparently at large, and in this fog was likely to remain so for a considerable time. But in the meantime, the monster that Brooking had created was holding Vivienne hostage.

Tern knew he could not return, for two reasons. Firstly, he was lost; and secondly, according to Duval, the cruiser was being watched — or at any rate, approaches to it. But he could not be sure on that last score. Duval might have been lying, or misinformed. He had to find out.

Slowly and laboriously, with many stops to listen for the shrilling of a whistle, he retraced his steps as best he could. The hooting of a ship's siren gave him a line and saved him from going off in the opposite direction. At last he almost gave up, then suddenly realised he was standing at the entrance to the alleyway that had originally brought him up from the warehouse. Hardly daring to breathe, he started down the alley, his footsteps muffled by the fog and drowned by the medley of odd noises that permeated the air from a variety of sources.

The door to the boat-house was ajar, a fact that he did not notice until he was pushing it open. Then he became aware of a group of blue uniformed figures standing just inside, their voices a jumble of low-pitched sound. Tern halted abruptly, staring aghast over the heads of the police at where the cruiser had been lying in its basin.

It was no longer there.

For an instant he was paralysed, not knowing whether to feel relief or a harsher kind of fear. He guessed without being told that the monster had taken the cruiser from its berth, slipping silently out into the darkness and mystery of the river. But had it taken Vivienne with it? Or was her body even now bobbing sluggishly on the tide-rip somewhere out there beneath the backdrop of fog?

A figure crowded through the door at his back. A hand landed firmly on his shoulder and spun him round, to peer up at the disgruntled face of Pete Duval.

'And you, my old, old friend!' he snarled. 'If it wasn't for the fact that I love you as a brother, Jerry, I'd use a cosh on your bonehead skull!'

'Sorry about that,' grunted Tern miserably. 'You can have my hunch, pal. The monster, the Blue Peril, the half-man half-robot, has been and gone. I know because I was talking to it less than half an hour ago. And it's got Vivienne Conrad with it now!'

At the sound of the words the group of police closed in, a sergeant asking questions. He was quickly replaced by an inspector, also inquisitive. Tern found himself telling the whole story, and, to his surprise, being believed.

Within a few minutes the boat-house was heaving. From the foggy background of the river came the throb of an engine, and a river police launch sidled up. Beyond a quiet call between the men, everything went off with smooth, almost silent efficiency. Tern was informed that no vessel could move either up- or downstream without being checked and halted. And the fact that the cruiser could not have at the outside more than thirty minutes' start made the river men confident of arresting it.

But Tern was frantic about the unfortunate woman on board. He tried to impress on the police what would happen to her if the vessel was caught. They did not seem to appreciate the awful danger in which she stood. No trace had been found of Brooking; he had simply vanished in the maze of fog-bound London.

Tern and Duval managed to insinuate themselves on one of the river police launches. As it nosed away from the quay, Tern's eyes fell on neatly coiled rope, grappling irons, all the various paraphernalia so often used by these men to recover bodies and bring them to shore. His heart sank at their dumb significance, and the mournful noises of the river did little to raise his spirits.

The launch was ten minutes out, heading downstream at what seemed to Tern a snail's pace, when the radio operator called urgently to the sergeant in charge. Tern and Duval joined in, sensing important news. When they heard it, it was more important than either had expected. Three miles further down, Brooking's cruiser had been in collision with a tug and barge.

Tern groaned inwardly.

'The cruiser was travelling at a crazy speed considering conditions,' reported the operator. 'According to Number Three Patrol, it sank almost instantly.'

Tern licked his lips. 'And the crew?' he said grimly. 'The monster . . . ?'

'Number Three report no trace,' came the answer. 'But the master of the tug says he thought he saw something about the size of a small man swimming for the shore.'

The sergeant looked down his nose gloomily. 'It looks as if we can chalk up the woman as missing, believed drowned,' he grunted. 'Sorry, Tern; there's nothing we can do beyond the routine search for the body when it drifts ashore.'

Duval clapped a hand on his shoulder. 'Drop me at the next landing place, will you, Sergeant?' he muttered. 'Have to get a story in somehow.'

The sergeant nodded. Sirens hooted in the fog like a bevy of lost souls; the sullen splash of the river seemed to sound its requiem for the missing woman. Tern and Duval stood silent in the cockpit, staring through the whorls of moisture.

Then the radio operator was busy again, taking down a message. 'They've picked up the woman!' he announced in a pleased tone. 'The current carried her half a mile. She was in a lifebelt and was picked up by a lighter, wet but safe.'

Never, Tern realised, had he been so glad to hear anything before. Vivienne's safety had grown to be of immense importance to him. He acknowledged the fact without reserve, not shying from its implications in the least.

There followed a period of intense activity. Tern at last shook off Duval, joined Vivienne at the river police post to which she had been taken, and waited while the business of making statements and signing them was completed. He, too, had to add his own quota of information, and by the time it was finished the police were ready enough to accept the fact of the Blue Peril's existence. But a wide search had failed to discover the creature. It was still at large, and a menace to any community.

At long last Tern was able to prise

Vivienne loose from the police and take her to a quiet spot where they could both talk and eat at the same time.

'You know,' she said in a puzzled tone, 'that horrible thing actually saved my life. It doesn't seem possible, Jerry, but it did. When the cruiser crashed full tilt into that tugboat, I was thrown clean over the side. The tide was running fast and I didn't have a chance. I was being swept straight past the tug.'

He frowned. 'But how did it save you?'

'I'm telling you. I caught a glimpse of it getting ready to dive overboard; and then suddenly it stopped, turned round and picked up a lifebelt. Before I knew what was happening, it had thrown it straight towards me. Then it dived and disappeared.'

'For an inhuman monster like that, it was certainly a curious thing to do,' Tern mused. 'But then, if what we think is right, it has your brother's brain in that awful head. I suppose some trace of sympathetic feeling for you must exist in its thought reflexes. There's no other answer.'

Vivienne shivered uncontrollably. 'Oh, I hate to think of it!' she whispered. 'If only all this had never happened! If only Gregory had had the strength of mind to break with Brooking right at the beginning, instead of getting involved in murder!'

Tern regarded her steadily. 'We can't alter the past,' he murmured, 'but the future's a different thing. If I get a car, will you come out of town for the rest of the day and get away from all this? We could take a run out to the country — get this fog out of our lungs; relax completely.' He broke off with a grin. 'I'm unemployed, remember? My time's my own, which is useful.'

She was genuinely delighted, falling in with the plan at once. Within an hour, the two of them were threading their way through the suburbs, as free of care as if the Blue Peril had never existed except in their imaginations. And it seemed, too, as if the elements were on their side. Hardly had they cleared London before the fog thinned and lifted, to let down a pale sun on the autumn-brown leaves of the countryside.

Tern put himself out to take Vivienne's mind completely off the nightmare through which she had recently lived, and the fact that he succeeded beyond his wildest expectations gave him considerable pleasure. But at the back of his own mind was the knowledge that Brooking's hideous creation was still very much alive, a fact that was brought home to them forcibly when they learnt that another savage killing had taken place during the afternoon. A man, it appeared, had seen and attempted to stop the monster. He had died, his skull crushed by a tremendous blow.

Tern tried to keep the facts from Vivienne, but she, too, had been listening to the telling of them in a small country pub where they had stopped shortly after six. Her eyes were troubled again, and the colour went from her cheeks. Even the pleasure they had found in each other's company was wiped out and almost forgotten.

'Take me home, Jerry,' she whispered. 'It — it seems wrong to be out like this when that dreadful thing is killing people again. What can it hope to gain?'

'A sort of distorted revenge on the human race,' he said. 'You heard what it told us — that's its main objective.'

She sighed. 'Let's get going.'

Tern wished he could change her mind, but she was adamant. Driving slowly through the dusk, they started back towards town. Vivienne was quiet, subdued; Tern himself uneasy. He must try to make her forget, he thought. She must be made to realise that this thing was impersonal now as far as they were concerned. Their part in it was over and done; the police were better equipped to deal with the ravages of the Blue Peril.

Presently he stopped the car in a side lane and brought out a pack of cigarettes. Vivienne accepted one, watching his face in the flare of the lighter flame. And behind the worry in her eyes he read something else. Their cigarettes were never lit. At one moment they were staring at each other; the next she was crushed against him, half-crying, a child in the dark.

'It'll be all right, won't it?' she breathed.

'Of course it will,' he murmured, his

lips against her forehead. 'The only thing that matters is us. From now on it's you and me, Vivienne. This curse that entered our lives brought us both together. It'll leave us together. Nothing can alter that, sweet.'

She drew a shuddering breath. 'I — I think I'd like my cigarette now, please,' she whispered. 'I feel as if I want to stay here forever,'

He grinned in the darkness, fumbling again for his lighter. 'There are nicer places than this,' he said quietly. 'Here.' He flicked the lighter again, watching hungrily as she bent her head forward, the cigarette between her lips.

Then the car door behind her was wrenched open, and the bulbous head of the Blue Peril thrust into view.

'Don't move, Tern,' it said. 'There are still several reasons why I want you both.'

7

Courtship Deferred

Caught completely off his guard, Tern could do nothing. The space inside the car was not roomy enough for any heroics; and as Vivienne stifled a scream, he guessed that the monster was pressing a gun in her back. He himself was cramped by the steering wheel, so that he could only sit where he was and stare in a horrified fashion at the grinning visage of the thing that had crept upon them from the night.

'You show surprise at my arrival, Tern?' it said. 'No, Vivienne, don't flinch whenever I speak. In some small measure you have already experienced my high regard for you. You would only suffer if this young man — who I am certain is humanly attached to you — tried some foolish act of heroism. Such an act would be little more than your own passport to eternity.'

'How — how did you find us?' she

stammered faintly.

Tern gulped. 'Yes,' he said, 'tell us!'

The monster made no immediate answer, instead moving to one side and opening the rear door of the car. Before they realised what it intended, it was sitting on the back seat with its enormous ugly head between them. And the gun was in evidence just as Tern had guessed.

'I told you once before that I am endowed with a strange ubiquity of knowledge,' it said. The harsh, mechanical tones of its voice were softened slightly by a cynical banter. 'There is nothing I do not know if I put my mind to it — Conrad's mind, perhaps I should say. You have Brooking to thank for that, though I doubt if he ever realised what he was doing when he energised my frame and brought me to life.

'However, that is beside the point . . . The main fact is that I can concentrate on something and know all about it. Hence, Tern, when I began to feel the need for human company again, I merely thought about you for a few minutes. There was not much difficulty in reaching you once I knew where you were.'

Tern frowned. 'But look here, damn it,' he said, 'we haven't been parked in this lane more than ten minutes! By the news we had, you were miles away — committing another vile murder!'

The monster chuckled. 'That was several hours ago,' it murmured. 'I ought to have explained that I knew where you *would* be at a given time, which allowed me long enough to arrive here in a stolen car now parked among the trees over there. Have I answered your queries satisfactorily? If so, we can proceed.'

Tern swallowed again and wondered what the devil to do. He had never felt so utterly helpless in his life before, and the sensation was not a pleasant one. As for Vivienne, the little he could see of her expression in the gloom revealed stark despair. She sat there at his side, shrinking from the nearness of the creature behind her, staring beseechingly at Tern.

He reached out a hand and took her fingers, tightening his own on them in an effort to reassure her. Her hand was icy cold.

'What do you mean by proceed?' Tern

inquired. 'Haven't you done enough damage already? What hellish power drives you like this?'

'The power of hate, my friend. Hate for you and all your kind; hate for the man who created me through no fault of my own.'

'But why?' Tern was frankly puzzled. 'If you have the power of thought and reason, surely you can work out some compromise? Why make the whole human race suffer for the fact that you've been brought to life? What have *we* done to you, for instance?'

The hideous head was slightly bowed, almost as if its ponderous weight was too great for the small, slender frame that supported it. 'That is something I cannot answer, Tern. This hate that rides me is deep, sending me mad so that I am compelled to slay if the need arises. I do not want life, you understand; but now that I have it I shall keep it, punishing the mortal world for giving it to me.'

'I see . . . And us, Vivienne and I? Where do we figure in your plans?'

Again the monster was silent for a space.

'Has it dawned on you,' it murmured, 'that so far you are the only human beings I have spoken with at any length? I am almost inclined to look on you as friends — if such things exist. I've been hunted and hounded like an animal. Even now the police, working in co-operation with the military, are trying in vain to follow my trail. You, on the other hand, have learnt that it is best to show me no violence. You have that in your favour; and the fact that Vivienne's brother died to give me life may be something to do with it as well. The fact remains that I do not *want* to kill you. Such a course would only be forced on me by circumstance. Not that I should hesitate, of course; but those are my sentiments. Of all human lives, yours are probably the only ones that have any tangible meaning to me. That is all I can tell you.'

Tern considered thoughtfully. It seemed incredible that this man-made being could discuss such things so lucidly. He began to wonder if it really understood its own feelings. And wondered, too, what he himself could make out of them. If there was a weak point in the monster's armour, he must find it at all costs. Their very lives would eventually depend on overcoming it.

The creature interrupted his train of thought. 'Now that we know a little better where we stand, Tern, you will oblige me by starting the engine and driving this car exactly where I tell you to. Do not forget, either, that at the first sign of a trick I shall use this peculiar weapon on Vivienne.'

Tern elbowed round, facing the front. His jaw was grim, and he was horribly aware of the thing that sat behind him. Aware, too, of Vivienne's silent terror at his side.

He pressed the starter button and throttled up, then glanced over his shoulder at the shadowy form of their uninvited passenger. 'Where to?' he demanded curtly. 'And what happens if you're spotted in the back through no fault of mine?'

'You will drive towards London and turn off when I tell you to. As for the rest . . . I hope for Vivienne's sake that we are not stopped. I can look after myself.'

Tern scowled, selecting second gear and letting in the clutch. He picked up the main road a short time later and drove at a steady thirty, blessing the darkness, for it prevented the Blue Peril from being seen. Vivienne sat tense at his side, hardly daring to move a muscle. Tern stared ahead through the windscreen, driving with all the caution he knew.

'Take the next fork on the left,' came the brief command. 'It is what you call a secondary road. Seven miles along it you will come to a garage. Stop there. I shall be out of sight underneath this rug so thoughtfully provided by the hirers. You would be well advised not to draw anyone's attention to me.'

'Why stop at the garage, then?' Tern asked.

'Because you will need a full tank of petrol; there is a long drive ahead of us.'

Tern did not inquire how the monster knew of the garage, nor how it knew so much about the countryside as to navigate without a map. There was no need to ask because he already knew the answer. This creature was omniscient if it chose to use its powers. There was a wealth of terror in the endless possibilities opened up by that single realisation.

Tern began to pray that before long something would happen to bring an end to it all. He even toyed with the notion of crashing the car in the hope of throwing the monster off its guard for long enough to overcome it. Only the risk to Vivienne, and a sneaking doubt in his mind that he could move swiftly enough, deterred him from trying.

The garage loomed in sight ahead, just as he had been informed it would. He glanced over his shoulder. There was no sign of the monster beyond a humped shape under the travelling rug. But a small, tense hand thrust Brooking's automatic through the narrow space between the two front seats.

'Fill up with petrol and behave quite naturally, Tern,' came the whispered order.

He gave a curt nod. A tow-headed youth appeared in the lighted forecourt of the garage as he stopped in front of the pumps. Tern glanced at the fuel gauge; the tank was half-full.

'Petrol, sir?' inquired the youth politely.

'Four please,' said Tern. From the sound of his voice it was impossible to tell that he was doing anything more than taking his woman out for an evening. But his mind was a turmoil as he struggled with the problem facing him.

The youth started one of the pumps, leading the hose to the filler cap. Tern was thinking fast, appearing relaxed. He felt the pressure of Vivienne's knee against his own. She was quivering like a fettlesome horse. Then the whirr of the pump ceased and the youth came round to the driving side.

Tern felt for his wallet, racking his brains for some way of making their plight understood without letting the monster realise it. In his heart he knew there was none. And then he discovered with a shock that his wallet was missing.

Tern felt himself growing hot under the collar. He was searching his other pockets frantically now, but there was still no wallet. He only had some loose change in his trousers. Helplessly, he shot a glance at Vivienne. 'Have you got any money on you?' he said uneasily. 'My wallet's gone!'

'I haven't!' she gasped.

The youth eyed him suspiciously, growing restless. 'You mean you can't pay?' he said flatly.

'You'll have to take my name and address and trust me. I had several pounds, but I've lost my wallet. Can't think where.'

'We've had your kind 'ere before,' the youth said bleakly. 'That's an old dodge, that is.' He stood close, but Tern saw him reach behind and press a bell-push three times in rapid succession. The trouble signal, he thought desperately. At any moment someone else, someone prepared to deal with shysters, would appear.

'Where do you think you lost it?' asked the youth. 'Is it on the floor, or between the seats, or in the back?'

He's keeping me talking till help arrives, thought Tern. And then to his horror the youth produced a large flash-lamp and turned on a brilliant beam of light, shining it straight into the car.

Tern acted instinctively, not waiting to consider the consequences. He had kept the engine running. It was the work of an instant to snap into gear and drive off with a violent lurch. The youth yelled some unintelligible string of invective that was drowned by the noise of the exhaust. Then the car was bounding down the road flat out as Tern pressed it hard through the gears. At any moment he was terrified he would hear the crash of the Blue Peril's gun in a vengeful shot. Instead the creature threw off the rug that had covered it and leant over the back of the seats.

'You are a fool,' it said coldly, 'but that action was at least commendably rapid. I need hardly say that it saved that person's life in the bargain — a small point to me, but more important to you. It also undoubtedly saved Vivienne. You may now proceed according to plan.'

Tern compressed his lips angrily. 'Before long we shall have the police on our tail!' he snapped. 'You don't think that yokel and his friends will let us get away scot-free, do you? They'll be on the phone by now, and the odds are that he took our number as we left. He wasn't all that dumb! You'd better think fast and make it good!'

'I am already doing so,' came the answer. 'Take every turn I tell you to. We shall avoid all police activity in that way. And drive as fast as you can.'

Tern needed little encouragement. They raced on through the darkened side-roads, twisting this way and that at the direction of the Blue Peril. It was incredible how the creature did it, but certainly by the end of an hour they had seen not a soul on the roads, let alone a searching police car or checkpoint.

'I think the danger is over for the time being,' said the monster quietly. 'And what is more, we have gained a lot of mileage in the right direction. You may now slow down a little and relax your nerves.'

Tern was completely lost; he had no idea where they were or where they were heading, so often and so sharply had they altered course during the last sixty minutes.

'Where are we going?' he demanded irritably. 'If you're involving us in your plans, you might as well be more communicative about them.'

The hideous being leant forward between them so that Tern could see the electrode terminals on its neck and the gleam of the dash-lamp on its shining skull. He suppressed a shudder.

'We are almost at our destination,' it said. 'You human beings seem to lack patience to an appalling degree.'

Tern went on driving. They were right out in the open country, fifty miles from London for all he knew. It was a long time since he had glimpsed a signpost, and even then had been too busy to read it.

Presently he was told to stop. He saw a white-painted gateway alongside the selected place. A rough, unkempt drive angled off into the darkness. The monster peered out through the side window. Tern braced himself, but before he could strike, it turned its head and smiled sardonically.

'Don't try anything,' it warned. 'Your thoughts are transparent. I keep a check on them occasionally.'

Tern said nothing; he was too depressed. His eyes met those of Vivienne as she stared at him helplessly.

'Drive up that track till you come to the house,' ordered the monster quietly.

Tern did as he was told; he had little choice. About a hundred yards up, standing well back in a spinney of trees, was a two-storey farmhouse, gabled and half-timbered with ivy thick on its chimneys as they climbed to the sky.

'Draw up in front of the door, Tern. Keep the engine running.'

The house appeared to be in darkness. Tern stopped and waited grimly. His heart was racing, and he wondered what was coming next. Whose house was this? Why were they here?

The monster opened the door and stepped out, standing by Vivienne's window. Then he opened her door and grasped her by the arm. She gave a little cry that was bitten off short. Tern twisted round and across, only to find himself facing the gun.

'My hostage — my safety precaution, Tern,' murmured the monster. 'I am going to leave you in the car for a few moments. Vivienne will go with me while I complete what I have to do. If you stay here and do nothing, she will come to no harm. Otherwise . . . '

He and Vivienne started away from the car, passing in front of the radiator, heading for the front door of the farmhouse. Tern was helpless. He put his head out of the window and called: 'Wait! I'd rather come with you!'

The monster, dimly seen in the gloom, paused. 'You will remain where you are,' it said flatly.

Tern stared miserably at Vivienne's figure beside that of her captor. It did not appear to be hurting her, but retained its grip on her arm so firmly that she had no chance of breaking away. And then they had reached the door, and the being was turning the handle. The door was locked. A distant pealing of a bell from somewhere inside told of what was happening. Presently a light gleamed in the window nearest the door. A moment later there was a clatter as a bolt was shot back.

Light spilled out across the porch. Framed in the half-open door was the shawled figure of an old woman. Tern heard a gasp of fear, then the monster had shot out a hand and stifled it before it rose to a scream. The old woman sagged weakly against the door jamb, slipping to the ground unconscious.

So incensed was Tern that he started to leave the car. But the monster looked back over its shoulder. The light shining on its face was sufficient to remind Tern of Vivienne's plight. He sank back in his seat and cursed at his own impotence.

Vivienne was thrust through the doorway with the monster close on her heels. The crumpled shape of the old woman remained where she had fallen, senseless and pitiful in the patch of yellow light from the door.

And from inside the house came a swift succession of noises that jangled Tern's nerves. A man cried out in open fear. There was a muffled report, like a shot being fired at close quarters. Furniture crashed, and Tern distinctly heard Vivienne scream. He was getting out of the car again when she appeared at the open doorway of the house.

She was sobbing brokenly, still firmly grasped by the monster. And the monster was dragging another figure behind it, a figure that struggled and thrashed about like a landed fish on a line. Not that its efforts at escape seemed to worry the monster in the slightest. The immense power of its artificial muscles seemed inexhaustible.

Tern opened the car door, peering narrowly to see who the latest passenger was likely to be. With an almost physical shock he recognised the pinched features of Brooking.

8

Night Operations

Brooking was forcibly bundled into the back of the car. He was in a state of gibbering terror. Vivienne took her seat beside Tern again. She was so pale he thought she would faint, but her fingers closed on his hand in a reassuring way. The Blue Peril insinuated its diminutive form into the back alongside Brooking. The great bulbous head and cold eyes seemed to fill the entire car with an atmosphere of pure malignancy.

'Turn the car and drive off,' came the sibilant command. 'Right on the road, first left, then first left again.'

Vivienne crouched in her seat, trying not to listen to the terrified mutterings of Brooking. The man seemed to sense that he was in dire peril, but was half-crazed in more ways than one. Tern kept his peace, grim-faced and full of hate for this being in whose power they were. The night road unwound before him as he followed instructions.

Brooking fell suddenly quiet for a space. Then there was a violent convulsion in the back of the car, a cry, and the sound of a sickening blow. Brooking was even quieter.

Tern glanced over his shoulder, to see the man slumped with his head lolling back against the seat squab.

'What foolish things fear puts into a man's head,' said the monster coldly. 'Imagine trying to overpower me. He will give no further trouble for some time now.'

'Have you killed him?' whispered Vivienne nervously.

'Not yet. Why do you think I went to the trouble of picking him up from his country hideout? Because I have other plans for his eventual disposal. My revenge will be complete when it comes. In the meantime he will remain with us — part of my circus of performing humans, one might almost say!' A thin, piping laugh came to them from the darkness. 'You have behaved very well so far, Tern,' the voice went on. 'Let us have no disappointments in the future.'

Tern permitted himself a cynical smile, unseen by his companions as the car took the second left hand bend. 'Our ideas of disappointment are slightly at variance,' he replied. 'Where are we going now? Or is this one of those 'mystery rides' so beloved by seaside charabanc proprietors?'

'Your levity is out of tune. You will continue to drive where I tell you to. And since we have a journey of several hours ahead of us, I suggest that you take it steadily and conserve your strength for what is to follow.'

'You're a sardonic devil, aren't you?' grunted Tern.

'The next right fork will take us to a trunk road,' said the monster quietly. 'We shall bypass London that way, going north. Carry straight on once you reach it. I will give you further instructions later on.'

It was one a.m. before Tern recognised approximately where they were. St.

Albans lay ahead; and beyond that the great northern arteries, now alive with their constant streams of heavy transport thundering to and fro like convoys on the move. But the monster had no intention of joining such a stream. Tern was directed to branch off, taking quieter secondary roads that were not so direct but led in the same general direction.

Tern was growing sleepy now. He only kept his mind on the road with an effort, realising that he had been on the go consistently for far too many hours without sleep. A sidelong glance at Vivienne showed that she had already succumbed. Her head lay sagged against the door beside her; her hands were limp in her lap, relaxed and at peace. He was glad, but wondered at the same time at the physical miracle that can come to the human body and bring release from strain when it reaches a certain pitch of exhaustion. He did not need to look at the monster to know that it never slept; that its vigilance was forever on the alert.

The car thrummed on through the night. Once the monster in the back told him to turn down a narrow lane. He did so obediently, not knowing the reason, but so tired that he was past caring.

'There is a police block along that other road,' the monster said. 'We are merely bypassing it.'

Tern summoned wakefulness enough to give a sour grin. 'You know all the answers, don't you?' he grunted. 'What happens when I fall asleep? Sort that one out!'

'You will not fall asleep,' came the answer. 'If you do, there will be an accident and Vivienne will die. Her life is in your hands, Tern.'

Tern grunted disconsolately.

'We have not much further to go now in any event,' went on the Blue Peril. 'You will hold yourself ready for any emergency. There is likely to be some slight difficulty in the near future, but I think we shall manage. Keep driving.'

Weariness sloughed off Tern's mind as he listened. What were they heading for?

The road unfolded in front, a grey ribbon in the flare of the headlamps. The car sped out from between long lines of fir trees. On one side now was a vast flat expanse of open land. Tern caught sight of a red flashing air beacon away in the distance. Then the bulk of a hangar showed up as well. The dark cluster of aerodrome buildings lay off to the left.

Tern furrowed his brow. This was a big R.A.F. bomber 'drome, he knew. Being a weekend pilot himself, the surroundings were far from strange. He could even hear the thunder of engines away in the distance as a kite warmed up for a training flight. And a new fear expanded in his mind like a balloon being inflated.

As if in answer to his unspoken questions, the monster said: 'Yes, Tern, this is our destination. You are no doubt very interested?'

'Just what do you mean to do?' he growled uneasily.

'Strike a more telling blow at your futile civilisation,' came the ominous reply. 'Out there at the end of the runway is one of this country's most powerful long-range bombers. It is fully loaded with live stuff, ready to take off for a practice flight and bombing exercise off the Scottish coast. All most convenient. It will not, of course, be flown by its normal crew, nor will its destination be as planned by the R.A.F. However, you will learn more of that presently. Keep driving, Tern; I have a feeling that we may meet some opposition further along the road. The authorities are singularly suspicious, guarding their aerodromes closely. It may be that some of the vigilance is increased on account of the reputation I am gaining. We shall see.'

Tern was cold with anger and helpless with rage. But the muzzle of the creature's automatic was pressing against the back of his neck, and the monster's arm was poised for a quick blow at Vivienne if he tried any tricks. He knew that blow, if it landed, would be enough to kill her. Mercifully, the woman herself was still in a deep sleep of exhaustion, unheeding of the danger now building up around her.

'Faster!' came the shrill command. 'Faster, I tell you, and do not stop for anything. Drive straight into the main entrance to the 'drome. I will direct you from there.'

Tern gritted his teeth in sheer desperation. Hunched over the wheel, he sent the car forward at flat-out speed.

He saw the road block when it was still a hundred yards away. A white bar lay across the road, with figures in a group on either side of it, dimly seen. Someone was waving a red lantern to and fro. They wanted him to stop. In the beam of the headlamps he made out the uniformed shapes of civilian police, R.A.F. regiment guards, and a few civilians in raincoats and felt hats. He saw, too, the gleam of rifles, and knew that there was trouble piling up.

'Straight through!' shrilled the monster. 'Do as I tell you, Tern. For Vivienne's sake, keep going. Smash the barrier!'

Tern ducked low, his foot flat on the floorboards as the car roared forward. He had often see this kind of thing done on the films; had never imagined he would one day do it himself — with a gun sticking in his neck.

Vivienne woke up with a scream as the first shot was fired at the racing vehicle. It starred the windscreen but passed harmlessly overhead. Then there was a shattering crash, and the car seemed to check momentarily as it met the heavy pole of the barrier. A cloud of steam shot upwards from the radiator. Men were shouting and cursing on all sides. Someone thrust an arm in through the open window beside Tern, attempting to seize the wheel. Then the car lurched free and was moving again with little apparent slackening of speed. The steam from the burst radiator obscured the windscreen so that Tern had to look through the side window. The shouting had stopped, but a rifle cracked venomously in the background. Then a veritable hail of bullets crackled past and over the lurching car. One ricocheted whiningly off the wing.

Vivienne had screamed only once; now she was huddled down on the floor beneath the scuttle, cowering from danger. The monster grasped her neck, keeping a hold on her. 'Keep going!' it snarled.

'She'll seize up in a minute or two!' Tern replied. 'The rad's burst!'

'Keep going, I say! It will take us far enough!'

At that moment Brooking decided to wake up. He at once started lashing out at the monster, only to be crushed again by another stunning blow on the head. And then the car gave a violent lurch as one of the stray bullets that flew around it found a mark in one of the tyres. The bang of the burst seemed to form part of the grinding, splintering crash that followed immediately afterwards. Slewing broadside, the careering car skated straight for a brick wall, struck it a violent blow and bounced off on another tangent, only to hit a shallow ditch and roll over on its side.

Tern fought the wheel till the last moment, conscious of being driven by that instinct for self-preservation that wipes out all other considerations. In those few fleeting seconds he forgot about the monster, Vivienne and Brooking; forgot even that his own countrymen were shooting at him.

Then his head shot forward as the car jolted into a ditch. His forehead met the rim of the steering wheel in a blinding impact and he sagged unconscious, no longer aware of what was going on around him.

* * *

'You'll be charged when we get you to the station,' said the police superintendent sternly. 'It's about time people like you were checked once and for all.'

Tern glared round the bunch of men who hemmed him in. They had lifted him from the car and carried him to the guard room close by the road block. That much was obvious, but a new fear came to him as he looked round for signs of Vivienne and the others.

'Listen, you damn blind fools!' he said tensely. 'Do you imagine that was my party? The Blue Peril was in that car, making me drive it. Haven't you got it yet? And where are Vivienne and Brooking?' He rubbed a hand over his aching forehead. 'Oh my God, if only you knew!'

'That'll be enough of that,' said the superintendent.

Tern glared at him angrily. 'What happened?' he asked. 'You might as well tell me; it won't make any difference now, because if that thing's still loose you won't catch it. Has anyone seen the woman who was in the car?' He looked round desperately, but met only the cold, hostile stares of uniformed men. Most of them carried side arms or rifles.

The police superintendent eyed him stonily. 'There were three other people in the car beside yourself,' he stated. 'You were rendered unconscious in the crash. By the time we arrived on the scene, the other three had escaped in the dark. What is this nonsense about a Blue Peril, and who were the other three passengers? You'd be wise to answer sensibly.'

Tern swallowed hard, clenching his fists in rage. If only these fools realised their danger! 'Tell me this,' he said grimly; 'there was a bomber on the runway a while ago. Is it still there, or has it taken off?'

Almost before he had finished speaking, the door of the guard room burst open and an airman staggered in. His face was covered in blood and his jacket was torn down the front. 'Some joker's taking Number Five!' he gasped. 'Quick!

The crate's all bombed up, and if — ' He stopped, falling sideways against the door frame and sliding to the floor, out for the count. Men crowded round him, asking questions, trying to wake him up again.

The superintendent whirled on Tern. 'What's going on?' he demanded curtly.

'I've tried to warn you!' Tern said. 'The half-man, half-robot created by Brooking — the thing that's been murdering people — was in that car. His plan was to take one of the station bombers and use it for heaven knows what devilry. Pull yourselves together and get out there to stop it. If you don't, it'll probably drop its load on London!'

The superintendent was confused for a moment. He was a police officer, not an R.A.F. one, and this sort of thing was a little beyond his normal scope.

The phone rang shrilly. One of the regiment men, the guard N.C.O., picked it up and listened. 'Cripes!' he said. 'You don't say! Er — sorry sir. Yes, of course! Now, sir, very good!' He slammed the receiver back and turned to the superintendent. 'Squadron HQ report that if

Number Five takes off unauthorised, it must be brought down at all costs — it's loaded with secret stuff, and they're scared that enemy agents are trying to make off with it!'

Tern heaved a sigh of relief. At least something would be done now, he thought.

And then, even while he was congratulating himself, the airman who had staggered in with the news came to enough to do some further talking. The 'joker' he had previously mentioned appeared to be a small man with an enormous head, and he had battered the handful of men working on the bomber into unconsciousness in a matter of moments. Only this particular man had stayed awake, though helpless. Then the 'joker' had carried two apparently unconscious bodies on board the aircraft and started to taxi it out.

Tern felt as if a bucket of icy water had been flung in his face. *Two unconscious bodies!* The creature was taking Vivienne and Brooking with it on this insane flight!

Before he could say anything constructive, the entire guard room was a bedlam of orders being given and acknowledged. A crash tender screamed to a halt outside. Three R.A.F. men rushed in; they were armed. The guard commander was on the phone again, red in the face, talking nervously to someone very senior to himself. In the distance outside, a siren was wailing the alarm.

And the night air throbbed steadily with the thunder of boosted engines. Tern grabbed one of the N.C.O.s by the arm. 'What are they going to do?' he demanded.

The man shook him off savagely. 'Shoot the swine down, of course!' he snarled. 'That's the emergency siren now. In three minutes flat there'll be a dozen jet fighters warming up. We'll show the bastards whether they can pinch a kite or not!'

Tern sagged away, breathing deeply. Shoot them down . . . In the din and confusion all round him, he suddenly realised that no one was taking any notice of him anymore. The door was a yard away. And outside, a jeep was standing with its engine ticking over, unattended.

'Close all roads to the 'drome!' the superintendent was saying busily. 'Throw a cordon round the perimeter!'

A squadron leader appeared, flying helmet in his hand. He was grinning wickedly — a cheerful-looking soul with the devil in his eyes. 'Bang on, what!' he said to no one in particular. 'Bit of battle practice, eh? Just the job!' He elbowed over and grabbed the phone, reporting his arrival to the duty pilot's office. 'You bet, old boy! Be right over. Yes, too true! Tell Carruthers to get her turning. That's right, old man; just got back from a dance to find this cooking up. Good eh? Nothing like it since the old days. Bye.'

Tern was thinking fast. Most of the noise in the guard room was drowned out by the thunderous roar of a heavy plane taking off. That would be the bomber, with the Blue Peril at the controls. He shuddered. A pity they couldn't have stopped it before now.

The debonair squadron leader was just leaving. He moved with considerable speed, his lazy manner cloaking a well-developed sense of urgency.

Tern decided the time had come to do something definite. He sidled to the door in the wake of the squadron leader. Everyone else was too busy to notice the fact. He and the squadron leader reached the jeep at the same time, boarding it together.

'You don't mind, do you?' said Tern affably. 'Someone's borrowed my car and left me stranded. Must have a word with the station commander.'

The squadron leader grinned and slipped into gear as Tern hunched forward in the seat at his side. 'You won't get far with old Sloppy-chops, brother! Proper terror, he is. You the police?'

'Connected with 'em. Special department. Er — did you say Sloppy-chops has this station? I knew him during the last flap.'

The squadron leader chuckled. 'Then you'll know what I mean about him! Where are you heading, by the way?'

'Dispersal point,' answered Tern. 'Checking up on something. We think there may be someone here who has no right to be around.'

'Ah! The master sleuth, what?'

144

Tern grunted. The jeep was bumping rapidly along now. Several hundred yards away, the flare path had sprung into a river of light. Silhouetted against it were the squatting shapes of jet fighters and the more bulky fuselages of bombers. Three tenders tore past in the opposite direction, loaded with armed men. 'Looks as if they're manning the ack-ack guns,' said the squadron leader interestedly. 'You don't know what this is really all about, I suppose? Or shouldn't I ask you . . . ?'

'We think an enemy agent has stolen one of the bombers; that's all,' Tern said. 'Orders are to stop it at all costs; even to shoot it down if need be.'

'That's what I was told myself. Wizard prang, what? Too bad about the kite, though. One of the latest. The bus drivers say it's a peach to fly.'

'There's a woman on board it now,' said Tern very quietly.

'Holy Mick! Do you mean that?'

'Unfortunately, yes,' said Tern. 'And I'm truly sorry about this, too.' As he spoke he brought his fist up from somewhere close to the floor of the jeep, aiming it straight at the fully exposed jaw of the squadron leader as the man turned an astonished face towards him.

The blow was a beauty, as accurate as a rifle bullet, and with almost as much latent power when it connected. The man grunted weirdly. The jeep swerved to the side of the road just as Tern grabbed the wheel and straightened it out. Then he reached across, heaved the senseless man aside and slid deftly into the driving seat himself. During the process, the jeep almost stopped and the squadron leader disappeared over the side with a dull thud, landing in the ditch. Tern was sorry about it, because he had liked the fellow and meant him no harm, but he needed the jeep in a hurry for his own reasons. It was lucky, he thought grimly, that he had only recently undergone a training course in the handling of the latest jet fighters. There were distinct advantages to joining the R.A.F.V.R.

Alone in the jeep, Tern headed fast for the dispersal point. Already the thin scream of the turbine engines was shrill in his ears. Men were running hither and thither — mechanics making final checks; armourers loading the cannon magazines.

Tern brought the jeep to a skidding halt near the closest of the fighters, the one at the end of a dozen-long line, all warming up with mechanics in their cockpits. Coming up at the other end of the flight was a tender. He wondered if it was bringing the pilots, men like the squadron leader, ready to kill a plane for the good of the cause — cool, calculating men with training to back their courage.

But Tern had little time to indulge his curiosity. The man in the cockpit of the fighter he had chosen was just clambering down, wiping his hands on a piece of waste. At sight of Tern he paused, leaning forward for a better view of the newcomer.

Tern had to work fast. Fortunately, any noise that was made would be drowned by the high-pitched whine of the jets. The mechanic was coming to meet him, puzzled by seeing civilian clothes instead of uniform.

Tern shouted something in the din of

noise. They were close to each other now. The twin-boomed fuselage was between them and the rest of the waiting planes. Tern vas ready for it now. As the mechanic came close to hear what he was saying, he struck — neatly, coolly, effectively. As the hapless mechanic collapsed at his feet, he darted forward, and a moment or two later was settling into the cockpit after kicking away the chocks from the wheels. The engine was ticking over gently, too slowly to overcome the brakes. He was all set for his desperate bid, and Vivienne's life depended on how he went about it.

9

Flare Path Take-Off

Men in flying kit were piling out of the tender further down the line. Tern tightened his mouth and checked the instruments, then gunned the motor and sent the Vampire rolling away from the line. He could see the illuminated take-off in the distance at the near end of the flare path. Out on the perimeter of the 'drome, a battery of searchlights was coming into action, probing the sky for any signs of the stolen bomber. But by now it was well on its way; and from the sound of it when it took off, Tern guessed with a sinking feeling that it was heading for London.

He thought of Vivienne, the bomb load, Brooking, and the hideous creature who was up there controlling it with that fearful omniscience that put nothing beyond its reach. How the night would end, Tern hated to think; but somehow or other he must get in touch with the monster and try to persuade it to change its plan before the guns grew hot and death and destruction marked the coming of dawn.

The jet motor screamed as he turned down the flare path. He saw men waving at him frantically; they knew now that this was another pirate flight. But he was still the first off the deck; still the first to take up the chase. The rest would be too busy to bother about him once they were in the air. Or so he hoped.

Cool now that he was on his own and in a plane, Tern made final checks, then throttled up and streaked down the flare path. Without circling the 'drome, he set a southerly course, driving full bore, guided by the distant glow of light in the sky that told of London; guided, too, by the spires of probing searchlights. On this trip there was no need for radar locating apparatus. Always to the south, the lights formed a beacon. And suddenly to the lights were added the tiny sparks of bursting ack-ack fire. As if by magic, every searchlight beam swung and concentrated in a cone.

Staring ahead, Tern saw the speck of silver caught in the mesh. The light boys were hot! He put the nose down a shade and drove the jet fighter for all it was worth, closing the distance rapidly. As he flew, he brought the radio into action, searching for a live band, and praying that he could contact the monstrous being.

The flak increased in intensity. Detachedly, Tern wondered what people were thinking. Did they realise the peril in which they slept? Had the news leaked out yet? He doubted it. He was close enough now to see the heavy bomber jinking and dodging amid the lights. And London lay ahead, still safe. But the flak was flaring all around the bomber, closer and closer as the gunners got the range. Tern had gained a lot of height. He was well above the harassed bomber now, diving towards it, not quite knowing what to do when he failed to contact it by radio.

Then the radio crackled, and he found that the monster was calling *him*!

'Go back,' it ordered, its voice shrill and thin on the air. 'Go back, or Vivienne will suffer for your madness. What do you think you can do to stop me from reaching my objective?'

Tern gritted his teeth. 'You fool!' he groaned. 'The fighters will get you if the flak doesn't! Can't you understand that that crate you're driving doesn't stand an earthly chance against jet fighters? For God's sake, if you value your own hide, jettison that bomb load and land anywhere. Better still, jump for it and turn the kite over the sea!' As he talked, he watched the silhouetted shape of the bomber diving and climbing, twisting and turning in the network of lights against the velvet dark of the sky.

'My destiny is my own, Tern,' came the cold reply on the radio. 'Interfere, and it will gain you nothing but the certainty of death for Vivienne.'

Tern was so close now that he could see the flicker of exhaust flame from the bomber's engines. He flew close alongside, gesturing wildly; helplessly. Then there was a swift stammer of flame from a gun turret forward. The monster, or possibly even Brooking, was firing at him!

Clinging to the bomber like a limpet,

Tern sought for some way of changing the lunatic mind that controlled it. Before he could do a thing, however, hell seemed to break loose from somewhere above and behind him. Streamers of tracer and cannon shell tore past, disappearing into the fuselage of the bomber. No matter how the big plane dived and jinked, it could not escape that deadly hail. Tern made out the shadowy shapes of three other fighters going in to the attack. He heard confused noises on his radio. The thin sound of a scream came over on the air from the bomber. It was a sound that turned his heart to water with anxiety, for it might well have been Vivienne mortally wounded.

And then the air was full of diving, twisting shapes as the pack of jet fighters pounced on their kill. With two of its engines already out of action, the bomber laboured. Then it gave a lurch to port, sliding away in a savage slip, to fall from the network of lights, vanishing earthwards, a long plume of smoke and flame growing out from one of its wings.

Tern shut his eyes, loathing the visions

that creased his brain. He flew automatically, not caring now what happened to him. And from far below, down to where the twisting ribbon of the Thames gleamed faintly, down in the wake of the attacking fighters, there rose a great bloom of orange, a billowing mushroom of smoke and fire. Even as Tern saw it and watched against his will, it vanished, quenched in an instant as the mighty plane crashed into the river, killing its own funeral pyre. One by one the lights winked out, glowing red for a brief moment as the arcs slowly cooled.

Tern tried not to think of those last seconds on board the crashing bomber. But his imagination gave him little rest. He called on all his reserves of willpower in order to pull himself together and head the plane towards its base.

Only when he was within sight of the lighted flare path did it dawn on him that the moment he landed, he was due to be put under arrest again. It was not a prospect that cheered him; nor did he feel up to coping with official explanations and the innumerable questions he would have to face. There was too great a weight of misery on his shoulders for that. The only bright spot in the whole sequence of events had been the saving of London from bombing by the Blue Peril. Well, the Blue Peril was finished now. Nothing could have lived in that holocaust that had flared down from the sky.

Circling the aerodrome, Tern saw the last of the other fighters land along the lighted strip of the path. Then it was his own turn, and he had to make up his mind. He could have crash-landed in a field and chanced his neck, but that would mean wrecking the plane. It might be better to face the music after all. But instead of touching down on the main length of lighted strip, he brought her down right at the extreme windward end, braking hard and stopping short, long before he was anywhere near the buildings and dispersal point.

He switched off, finding to his joy that so far no one had even started towards him. He still had a chance to get clear and avoid the embarrassment of arrest — to say nothing of the righteous indignation with which the squadron leader would view him when they met again! *That,* he thought, would take a lot of living down.

He was thinking most of these things as he ran at full pelt towards the perimeter track, at this point backed by a stand of dark pines and forested scrub. His main object was to lie low for a while before making a break and getting back to London somehow. Now that Vivienne was dead and the monster finished, he would have to go to work again to keep his mind off recent events. He might even get his story accepted by his old editor before the police caught up with him.

★ ★ ★

The morning was raw, damp, and matching his mood when he arrived at his lodgings and put on a kettle for tea. The time was nine-thirty. By devious ways he had succeeded in evading capture at the aerodrome; had then borrowed a car without the owner's consent, abandoned it somewhere south of St. Albans, and taken an early-morning train. Now he was so tired that he doubted if he could keep awake for a minute longer.

Even if the police came and arrested him soon, it would be worth it to sleep for an hour. Memories of the recent tragedy swept his mind, reinforced by the account he had read in the newspaper. No bodies had as yet been recovered from the debris in the river. Wreckage had been scattered over a wide area, for it appeared that the bomber had exploded shortly before hitting the water. Mercifully there were no civilian casualties, and it was assumed that the only persons killed were the crew of the machine itself. For some reason or other, no mention was made that the plane might have been flown by the so-called Blue Peril.

'They probably didn't believe me even when my story was confirmed by that mechanic,' grunted Tern. 'What the hell, anyway?' He hurled the paper aside, poured himself a cup of tea, and sank into a reverie as he stared at the floor.

The phone in the hallway outside the door rang, breaking in on his sober thoughts like a fire alarm. For several seconds he took no notice of it, waiting for someone else to answer it. No one did. He dragged himself to his feet and slouched to the door. The phone was still ringing.

'Hello?' he said tersely, not giving his name for obvious reasons.

'I'm glad you answered, Tern,' came a shrill, piping voice. 'I was afraid you might let it ring.'

Tern's knuckles were white as he gripped the handset. He had to lean against the wall to support himself, so watery did his legs feel at the sound of that cursed voice again. 'I thought you were finished,' he muttered. And then a swift surge of renewed hope welled up inside him. 'You must have jumped! Did — did Vivienne get out in time?'

The Blue Peril chuckled on an ugly note. 'She did,' it replied. 'That is why I am contacting you. Listen to what I say and act on it. If you have any human feelings for this woman, you will come to where I am as quickly as you can. Bring bandages and some general first-aid equipment.'

Tern gulped. 'For God's sake, tell me if she's badly hurt! Where are you?'

'Keep your voice down, Tern! There is no need to lose your head. I know it was not you who shot us down. If it had been, Vivienne would have paid for your folly before now. As you guessed, we were all able to jump, though Brooking was unconscious at the time. I still take great care of him, you see? His time has not yet come to die.

'Fortunately, everyone imagines we were all killed. That is not the case, though you will be doing your friend a great service by bringing the first-aid kit. Are you prepared to do that without pulling any tricks? Once again, the woman is my safeguard and guarantee of your co-operation; never forget that, Tern.'

Tern gritted his teeth. 'Of course I'll come, damn you!' he snapped. 'Only tell me where you are!'

'Some distance from where we landed. We persuaded Brooking to drive. Later, of course, we abandoned the car and concealed it, proceeding on foot.'

'*Where are you?*' insisted Tern frantically.

'In a disused hutted camp among the trees of what is known as Epping Forest,' came the answer. 'Drive north out of the town till you come to a lonely phone box at a fork. It is the only one in that particular district, so you can't miss it. I can allow you two hours. If you fail to arrive by then, I shall take my revenge on Vivienne.'

'Is she with Brooking now?' Tern had an awful vision of Brooking treating her sadistically.

'Brooking has been rendered unconscious again, I regret to inform you. He is a violent man in his terror, subject to savage attempts on my life, which do not suit me. Bring the supplies for *her* sake, Tern. You are sure you can find the place?'

Tern ran over the details carefully, forcing himself to keep calm. He got more exact location details and prepared to ring off.

'Oh, just a moment,' said the sibilant voice. 'You had better leave your lodgings quickly. Use the back entrance. The police are coming towards the front door now. Hurry!'

'Damn your eyes!' snarled Tern. But he knew too much of the creature's amazing clairvoyance to discount the warning. In less than thirty seconds he had grabbed his hat and raincoat, ducked swiftly through the rear premises, and sprinted along the quiet street that ran at the back of the block. Whether anyone saw him leave, he did not bother to find out; but when he turned a corner some distance away and crossed the road on which his lodgings fronted, it was to catch a glimpse of two uniformed figures standing stolidly at the front door as they waited for admittance.

'I can thank the Blue Peril for that much at any rate!' he muttered. The news that Vivienne was alive was the best he had had in years, and even the fact that she was injured did not belittle his thankfulness.

Once clear of his own neighbourhood, he paused to work out a plan of operation. Luckily, he had remembered to cram a few notes in his pocket before leaving, so was well equipped to buy what he needed and hire another car. He decided ruefully that the car-hire game must be a very chancy one with customers like himself. It was doubtful if his next one would be returned at once. Anything might happen to it, if last night's adventure was a sample of the Blue Peril's brand of entertainment.

He hired a big American saloon from a small mews garage, filled up the tank, and drove off. Buying the first-aid equipment was not so easy, because he did not know what manner of injury they would have to deal with — the Peril had refused to say. In the end he stocked up with bandages, iodine, lint and all the usual household remedies for cuts and burns, which were the kind of injuries he thought Vivienne was most likely to have suffered.

It was exactly an hour and forty minutes after the monster had phoned him that he slowed the car and stopped near the phone kiosk in Epping Forest. A thin drizzle of rain was falling, and what little traffic used the road was all in a hurry. He got out of the car and stood peering round, wondering in which direction the hutted camp lay. There was no indication from where he was. Instinctively, he struck off through the trees to the right of the kiosk.

Hardly had he covered twenty yards before he stopped dead in his tracks. Right across his path lay the twisted body of a man, the flesh hideously torn and savaged. Tern shuddered, knowing by what he saw that he had found the right place. This killing was the monster's work. He dropped to his knees beside the still and horrid figure. Life was extinct, as he knew it would be. A tiny sound made him raise his head and peer round.

'The fool tried to intercept me,' said the monster quietly.

Tern bared his teeth angrily. The monster was alone for the first time, without Vivienne to threaten! He threw himself forward, lashing out with all his strength at the bald, gleaming skull and ugly face. But he might as well have attacked a shadow. The creature swayed backwards, seizing him by the throat with one hand and lifting him clean off the ground, right above its head as it heaved.

Tern let out an involuntary yelp of terror, half-choking in his throat at the awful pressure of those steely fingers. Then the monster flung him down and away, much as a child might toss aside a rag doll in a fretful temper. Tern landed heavily, the breath knocked from his body by the force of the impact. As he struggled to a sitting position, the blue-toned being was beside him with an agile leap. Its hand fell on his shoulder, lifting him upright and whirling him round despite his struggles.

'Had you been anyone else, you would have suffered more grievously,' it said in a bleak, high whisper. 'Will you never learn that it is dangerous to attack me?'

Tern said nothing, cursing himself for not trying to get hold of a gun before leaving town. Had he had one with him now, he would not be in this position. But again, recrimination was a waste of time.

'Behave yourself in future,' came the cold advice. 'I am liable to lose my temper once and for all with you, Tern.

Walk in front of me now, straight through the trees.'

Tern glanced venomously at the thing, surprised to see that it was holding the automatic in its right hand. Till now it had not bothered to display it.

The pair of them proceeded in silence for nearly a quarter of a mile before the first rusty hump of a Nissen hut showed up at the edge of a clearing among the trees.

'Not this one; the next one,' said the monster. 'We shall be joining the others in a moment now.'

Tern hesitated. 'The first-aid stuff!' he gasped. 'I left it in the car. What about it? Is Vivienne badly hurt?' All the old anxiety flooded buck into his mind, till now swamped by the tussle he had had with the monster.

The monster smiled — or rather gave that horrid twist of its face that passed for a smile. 'She will need no first aid, Tern,' it replied sardonically. 'Nor will Brooking. I had to bring you scurrying here, hence my playing on your emotional sympathy for the woman.'

'You devil!' Tern grated. And yet he felt relief seep in through the mist of his anger. Vivienne was safe and well, which made everything else worthwhile.

They stopped at the door of a ramshackle Nissen hut well screened by scrub and undergrowth against a background of trees. The windows were broken and the door hung drunkenly on one hinge. Tern thrust his way in, with his captor close on his heels. The inside was gloomy and damp-smelling, with grass growing up through cracks in the concrete floor. At the far end, two motionless forms were huddled against the curving wall. Tern ran towards them.

Brooking was unconscious; Vivienne bound and gagged. But her gaze was eloquent when Tern bent over and raised her gently.

The monster stood watching, cynical amusement quirking its mouth. 'You may release her now,' it said. 'I had to tie her while I met you; that was the only reason.'

Tern glanced round. He was between Vivienne and the monster, but the gun was aimed at his back; and to force another struggle would be suicidal.

The monster nodded slowly. 'A wise decision, Tern,' it murmured. 'I know your mind. But be quick and free the woman. There is work to be done, and I am anxious to carry out a further plan designed to throw your race into chaos.'

Tern did not bother to answer; if the monster could read his most intimate thoughts, it would know what he would have said had he spoken. Instead, he untied Vivienne and released the gag from her mouth. She whispered something to him, gripping his arm in quiet gratitude. The monster allowed them to talk and whisper for a moment or two before interrupting, but they had had time to say the kinds of things that are timeless.

'Come!' it said at length. 'Enough of this drooling! We will use the car now hidden among the trees not far from here.' As it spoke, it bent and picked up Brooking, tucking the scientist under its arm like a bundle of rags. The man might have had no weight for all the effort it seemed to need.

'Another crazy drive?' said Tern. 'It's

daylight this time. Aren't you asking for trouble?'

'The distance is so short that the risk will be negligible. You need have no fear; I know exactly what I am doing.'

'Just as you did last night, I suppose?' Tern's voice was bitter when he remembered the flaming torch of the crashing bomber.

'A slight matter of underestimating my enemy, Tern. It is not a mistake I shall make again, I promise you. Now you will walk ahead of me. I am holding Vivienne by the arm, and at the slightest sign of treachery on your part I have only to jerk sufficiently hard to tear it off. Do we understand each other?'

Tern faced him squarely. 'You know what I'm thinking!' he snapped. 'I'll do as you say because I have to; for no other reason.'

Vivienne shot him an imploring glance. 'Please,' she murmured, 'please, darling, don't take a chance. No matter what happens, don't risk getting hurt yourself. I'm all right, honestly I am.'

'Very well,' he said reluctantly. 'What

are we going to do?' he demanded of the monster.

The creature's eyes narrowed slightly. 'I feel it best to keep my own counsel on that point, Tern. All you need to know is that very shortly we shall take to the air again; but not, this time, in a loaded bomber. Now do as I have told you, and walk to the car.'

10

Hostile Reception

Just as the monster had promised, the ride was a brief one. Not far from the hutted camp, situated on the fringe of the forest, was a small maintenance aerodrome. Viewed in the thin, depressing drizzle of cold rain that was falling, the place had a forlorn, deserted appearance. Tern brought the car to a halt as directed, not by the main entrance, but up a narrow lane that flanked the field on the north.

'Aren't you a bit optimistic about getting a plane from here?' he said sourly. 'From the look of it I should say the field is closed.'

Vivienne stared unhappily from the car window. Brooking was still unconscious, a limp sprawl on the back seat beside the Blue Peril.

'That is where my ability to know

things is of such use, Tern,' came the answer. 'There happens to be an aircraft due to land here within a few minutes, In the present state of wind and flying conditions, it will come down close to where we are, then taxi round right past here. All we have to do is be ready to intercept it and take over.'

Tern grunted, wondering how the creature imagined it would be done.

As if in answer to his doubt, the thing went on: 'I am going to try something — a little experiment that I feel sure will prove most effective.'

'What are you planning now?' Tern growled

'Wait and see! It is curious, but I am only beginning to realise my own potential powers, developing them as I go. First it was my physical strength — a great asset. Then I discovered that very little was hidden from my knowledge if I cared to concentrate sufficiently on a subject. I am able to foresee things and events, as I have already proved to you in the matter of the police arriving at your London lodging. And now . . . '

'Now what? I suppose you'll tell us you don't need food or air to breathe!'

The monster gave its short, shrill chuckle. 'That, I think, is beyond my powers,' it admitted. 'No, this is even more useful — if it is effective. We shall see . . . ' It broke off. Then: 'You know, Tern, I find a certain pleasure in your company — a definite sense of amusement in watching your reactions to what I do and say. You're such a typical being of your race: stupidly courageous when timidity would be safer, and timid when a quick stroke of genius might alter your plight. You interest me; I should miss you if anything happened to you. The same does not quite apply to Vivienne somehow. With her I feel some vague affinity that prevents me from killing her unless the need arises. I suppose it is because we are a queer kind of brother-sister combination.'

Vivienne gave a shuddering sob and buried her face in her hands. The sight of her misery moved Tern to anger. He swung round, glaring at the monster and framing some remark, trying to measure the chances of another mad attempt at overcoming it.

The monster merely chuckled, then held up its arm. 'The aircraft, I think,' it said. 'We will wait by the fence.'

An atmosphere of tension gripped them as they left the car and stood in the drizzle, listening, watching the grey sky for a glimpse of the incoming plane. When it appeared, Tern recognised a civilian six-seater. It circled the field, then made its landing run almost directly towards the spot at which they stood. As it rolled to a stop, Tern held his breath, watching it curiously.

What new form of devilry had the Blue Peril thought up this time? The aircraft, a twin-engine job, taxied closer to the fence, then stopped again. Tern glanced shrewdly at the monster where it stood on the other side of Vivienne. Brooking had been left insensible in the car. The eyes of the monster were half-closed, focused on the aircraft, now stationary less than fifteen yards away. But it still retained its deadly grasp on Vivienne.

Suddenly the cabin door opened and

two men jumped to the ground, leaving the engines ticking over as they walked towards the fence, their faces curiously blank and dull.

Tern frowned. He knew that the men must have seen the incredible monster standing there, yet there was not even a show of surprise on their faces, let alone the fear or horror it usually instilled in people.

'It works even better than I expected, Tern,' said the monster. Its voice was low and tense, tinged with almost human excitement.

'What do you mean?' he grunted wonderingly.

'I am controlling these two men from a distance. They left the plane and answered my summons obediently. Now the field is clear for our own purpose.'

Vivienne glanced at Tern, then back at the monster. 'But what about them?' she whispered nervously. The two men, both young, had halted in front of the fence, staring at the little group with scant interest. It was as if they were awaiting the order to move on.

The Blue Peril considered for an instant. 'I could kill them and be sure,' it mused. 'Or I could merely send them away — up into the forest, for instance.'

'Don't kill them!' begged Vivienne urgently. 'Please, don't kill them! There's been too much of it! They have not harmed you; they've helped you by obeying you. Don't kill them for your own amusement!'

The monster smiled a little, its horrible mouth twisting. 'You have a kind heart,' it sneered. 'But I will humour your weakness. The men shall be spared. But we waste time. Tern, you will act as pilot on this occasion. It will suit me better that way. Can you handle that craft well enough to keep it airborne?'

'I imagine so, damn you!' He glared at the two men standing patiently on the other side of the fence. The monster lifted Vivienne up and over the fence with the ease of a giant, lowering her as lightly as a feather on the other side. Then it glanced at Tern.

'Go and drag Brooking from the car and bring him here,' it ordered curtly. As it spoke, it jumped over the fence and stood holding Vivienne's arm. Tern glared, but moved off obediently to the car. By the time he returned with Brooking, the two pilots were ambling slowly off through the sparse trees, not looking back, uninterested in what was going on.

The Blue Peril had added another trick to its repertoire, that of being able to direct people from a distance and make them do as it wished. Tern was not sure what the outcome would be, but decided that this latest development represented further danger to the community at large. He hoped the creature would not use its new power on himself or Vivienne.

They all entered the aircraft, with the monster always at Vivienne's side, a constant threat to Tern. Brooking was dumped in one of the aft seats; Tern took the controls.

'Take off,' he was ordered. 'I will give you further directions presently.'

Tern merely nodded. He saw someone walking slowly up from the direction of the aerodrome buildings in the distance.

The man was in no hurry, it appeared. He was probably a little curious as to why the aircraft had stayed where it was instead of taxiing down to the hangars.

A few minutes later they were in the air. Tern kept the plane climbing straight into the wind, getting the feel of it, settling down. There was plenty of fuel in the tanks and the engines droned perfectly. 'Where to?' he asked briefly.

The monster glanced over his shoulder. Then to his surprise, it gave him a compass bearing without hesitation. 'That'll take us out over the North Sea!' he exclaimed.

'Exactly, Tern. Carry on, please, with no argument. I have formed my plans. This country of yours is too crowded, too full of inquisitive fools who hamper my efforts. We are bound for foreign lands from which I can operate more easily.'

Inwardly, Tern groaned. This was going to be far more complicated than he had expected. What adventures lay ahead of them he dare not think, but almost certainly they were bound to run into trouble — unless the Blue Peril had means of quelling it and protecting them from enraged

177

foreigners. Would its undoubted powers be up to such a crisis? Tern did not know what to think.

The plane thrummed on across country. By now its behaviour would probably have been reported, unless it had been expected to take off again at once. They saw no other aircraft, but during the afternoon Tern mentioned the fact that before long they would need more fuel.

'You have enough to reach the landing ground I have selected,' the monster told him flatly. 'We shall refuel there and carry on. You may leave things entirely to me.'

Tern muttered something beneath his breath. It seemed a far cry from his usual life as a news reporter; he began to get nostalgic ideas about how pleasant London was. This present state of affairs was like living in a constant nightmare.

The cold grey of the North Sea slid away below, glimpsed through breaks in the cloud above which they flew. The line of a distant coast appeared, with a cluster of grey buildings to tell of a town or seaport. Tern, keeping to the original compass course, saw that they were making straight towards a small landing ground just inland from the flat coast.

'Land normally,' he was told. 'No one will get out, but a petrol bowser will come to us with fuel. I am hoping that my control will be sufficiently strong to make the staff do as they are told and then forget that we ever landed.'

'At any rate, you're a born optimist,' observed Tern. 'For your sake, I hope it works.'

'I hope so, too — for Vivienne's sake, Tern.'

Tern was silent as he went in to land. Brooking, who had recently recovered his senses and been tied up by Vivienne on the monster's orders, started cursing them all in succession. No one took much notice. The undercarriage was down and the plane coming in for a landing. Tern sat tensely. Vivienne, her face pale and strained, looked out ahead. The monster kept a hand on her arm, and the automatic was trained on Tern's back as an added precaution.

A group of technicians stood around near the control building, watching idly.

From the looks of it this was a British-manned 'drome. Almost before the plane rolled to a standstill, a petrol bowser motored up alongside. Tern held his breath, but the wooden-faced man merely glanced in his direction and proceeded to pump fuel into the aircraft tanks. The whole operation was carried out in silence, no word being spoken. The cabin door was not even opened. And when it was completed, the bowser drove off.

'Uncanny!' muttered Tern. But he was greatly disturbed by the fresh possibilities opened up by the monster's remote control of individual human beings. The monster itself seemed to sense his unease, for it chuckled quietly.

'Before long, you will see that I can work a surprising number of changes in your civilised world,' it murmured. 'And now take off again without delay. We have many miles to cover before dark.'

Tern, depressed and resigned to this awful companion's whim, felt that no escape was possible. The whole of his personality seemed to have become subdued and passive, and even Vivienne's nearness failed to stir him to revolt.

Flying on a fresh course, they travelled north-east over forest, plain, swamp and tracts of agricultural land in geometric ploughed patterns. And then, with the coming of dusk, they met their first opposition.

Tern was not sure over what country they were flying, but he had an idea that it was one of a group more or less at permanent variance with Great Britain. He had been expecting trouble for the last hour or two, and was not really surprised when his keen eyes made out the small fast shapes of a pair of low-winged monoplane fighters closing in on the aircraft from the side.

The monster, too, realised that a test was coming. It sat there immediately behind Tern, its small form hunched up in concentration, its evil eyes staring hard at the oncoming planes. 'Sent to intercept us and turn us back,' it commented.

'They'll shoot us down in the blink of an eye!' said Vivienne nervously. 'Aren't we running our necks straight into trouble?'

'They will not attack us,' the monster said firmly. 'I shall control them and overcome their pilots before they fire.'

'You hope!' Tern was very doubtful, and not a little nervous about the outcome. Even the demonstration at their last landing point had not entirely convinced him. The sight of these two potential enemies bearing down on them, bristling with machine-guns and cannons, was not an encouraging one. He held his course grimly, prepared to take evasive action at the slightest provocation or sign of open hostility.

The fighters ranged themselves one on either side of him, throttling back till they flew at exactly the same speed. He could see the faces of the pilots clearly, as well as the plane markings, the sight of which did not inspire confidence.

'You're a damn fool and you know it!' he threw over his shoulder at the monster.

'They're making signs to us!' gasped Vivienne.

Tern raised a hand and waved to the nearer of the fighters. There was no answering grin on the pilot's face; rather, the man's expression hardened ominously.

'What about your long-distance control now?' sneered Tern.

The monster said nothing, though whether from chagrin or because it was concentrating so hard, it was impossible to tell. Then without any warning, one of the fighters peeled off, coming in again at a tangent.

'Here it comes!' muttered Tern. As the first stream of bullets passed ahead of them, he thrust the nose down and dived the plane abruptly. The second fighter followed him down. Chips flew from one of the wings as a cannon shell tore its way across the port engine. Tern's face was white and set as he jockeyed the plane for all he was worth, diving and twisting like a fish in the sky. But he knew he was merely postponing the evil hour. However good he was, he could not hope to stand up to this kind of attack; and being unarmed itself, his own plane was helpless to retaliate.

The monster was muttering venomously to itself, dismayed at its own failure to hold off the enemy pilots as it had fully expected to do. Vivienne cringed down in her seat, clinging to anything she could lay a hand on for support as the aircraft bucketed about the sky. Brooking rolled off his seat and thudded onto the floor. He was screaming at intervals now, both from fear and madness.

Then there was a shock and a dull explosion. The plane pitched violently as a shell ripped into the starboard engine nacelle, breaking something with a heavy concussion. Tern fought desperately for control. A long streamer of black smoke began to curl and whip back from the damaged engine. It was out of action now, and the earth was making dizzy circles as it rose to meet the spinning aircraft.

How he ever managed it, Tern did not know; but when the plane was only a few hundred feet above the wooded snow-clad hills towards which they were spinning, he brought it onto an even keel and succeeded in holding it on a more or less straight glide. The second engine had failed by this time, and the plane felt heavy, slow to answer its controls. The port wing was flapping as if it were made of brown paper and might at any moment rip to pieces.

The two fighters were following the aircraft down, close on its tail. Tern could imagine the pilots with their fingers resting on the gun buttons, smiling to themselves. What a magnificent victory to report when they returned to base!

But his hands were full with the immediate needs of the moment. He dare not stretch the glide too much, yet the nature of the ground below was most inhospitable for a forced landing.

'There's a clear patch, darling!' cried Vivienne suddenly. She pointed across his shoulder, a little to one side of the line being taken by the staggering plane.

Tern had to make up his mind quickly. He might just reach it, he thought. It seemed very small, a tiny clearing among the trees, white with snow. What lay beneath the snow he could only guess. If there were jagged rocks, they would fare badly. But it was either that or the tree-tops.

Still conscious of the two fighters on his tail, he made a cautious turn, flattening out quickly. The clearing was very near now. He had too much height. He slipped it off neatly, dropping behind the screen of trees and touching the snow-covered ground. For a moment or two the plane floated on, reluctant to touch down, it seemed. Then there was a jarring thud, a flurry of churned-up snow, and the plane did a graceful nose-down ploughing manoeuvre before coming to rest with its forepart deep in a drift.

An appalling silence settled in the cabin. Then it was broken abruptly by a groaning cry from Brooking as his body catapulted down the gangway between the seats and crashed against the back of Vivienne's place. Luckily, Vivienne and her companions had had the presence of mind to fasten their straps, or else it might have fared badly with them. Tern could have wished that the monster had forgotten, but there was no chance of that.

'We've arrived,' he said grimly. He was so relieved at having got down in one piece after being shot up that he grinned round at the hideous face of the Blue Peril. And his hand reached out to Vivienne in a silent gesture of gladness.

'We must leave the vicinity before the wreck is investigated,' said the monster. 'I am disappointed that I could not control those pilots, but the explanation is a simple one.'

Tern frowned. 'How do you mean?' he grunted.

'They did not understand the language with which I was born; that is all. I tried to control them using thought impulses phrased in English. It was foolish of me, but a failing I shall quickly remedy when I have given their own tongue enough thought to absorb it. When we refuelled, the men there must have been English-speaking.'

Vivienne sighed unbelievingly. She still clung to Tern. He undid his straps and clambered towards the cabin door. Up above, he could hear the drone of the fighters. They were circling watchfully overhead, waiting like falcons to pounce.

'Open the door, Tern,' said the

monster. 'Head for the nearest cover.'

Tern swung round. 'We all leave together, damn you! Those swine will open up the moment we appear. Send Brooking out first, if you want a decoy to take the fire!'

They eyed each other warily. Then Tern was suddenly moving towards the door, opening it slowly, peering out and up at the slanting fuselage. He jumped to the ground, sinking to his waist in drifted snow. He was doing it all without thinking, acting on the unspoken command of the Blue Peril. And behind him he could hear Vivienne's broken cry as he left her. But somehow or other it made no difference.

He began to flounder through the snow, struggling to reach the closeness of the standing timber not far away, shivering with the cold that crept into his bones the moment he left the warmth and protection of the cabin. Less than ten seconds after he left the plane, the air seemed to crack with the whiplash of bullets. One of the fighters dived, firing as it came, intent on mowing him down.

188

Bullets kicked up the snow all round him, carving a trench to one side, spattering his face with icy crystals. He felt the fan of bullet wind. Then he flattened himself on the ground, cursing wildly. The hail of lead had missed him by bare inches. Now the fighter was zooming upwards again. The second machine had not yet positioned itself for an attack. Tern had a few moments' grace in which to reach the shelter of the tree-line.

Floundering along, he reached the trees just as the second fighter turned on the taps and smothered him in churned-up snow. He hurled himself forward the last few yards, staggering and gasping for breath as the boles of the trees at last gave him protection. And there he stayed, hugging the ground, feeling the bitter cold of this northern land enter right inside his flesh and bone.

He heard Vivienne crying out to him and looked up. Next instant, timing it beautifully between the two attacking planes, the monster appeared in the door of the cabin, holding Vivienne under one arm and the sagging form of Brooking under the other. It leapt far out from the plane, landing lightly beyond the drift in which Tern had floundered. Then it was leaping and thrashing its way towards him, making light of the trip, burdened as it was.

Tern found himself once again master of his own will and mind. Control had been lifted from him. He took Vivienne in his arms as the monster released her, hugging her close. But there was no time to pause and congratulate themselves on their escape. The two fighters, baulked of their prey, were raining cannon shells down through the trees. Branches were splintered above their heads; the air was made hellish by the stuttering bellow of the guns and the roar of the engines. Once again the monster seized Vivienne by the arm and started off through the forest, dragging Brooking along behind him. Tern was motioned on ahead. He was helpless to refuse, and life was becoming so difficult in the neighbourhood that an immediate withdrawal was advisable no matter who gave the orders.

By the end of ten minutes they were

well clear of the danger zone. Vivienne was showing signs of exhaustion, and Tern was ready to drop in his tracks. Only the monster showed no indication of physical collapse; its strength was inexhaustible. But it halted to let them rest, and to lower Brooking to the ground for a while, letting him sink in a shallow patch of snow that had drifted down between the trees.

Tern glared at it savagely. 'Well?' he grunted. 'You've landed us in a fine spot, I must say! What the hell do you think you'll gain from this recent manoeuvre?'

The Blue Peril smiled slightly. 'Our choice of landing place was surprisingly suitable,' it murmured. 'We are less than four miles from the very spot I should have chosen myself. All we have to do is cover that distance, and now that night is fast approaching our movements will be well concealed from unwanted witnesses. As soon as you are rested, we will proceed according to plan.'

Tern's mouth tightened. 'All I hope is that this time the plan's a more watertight one than your last! Come on.'

11

Broadcast Command

The monster did not deign to answer. Within a minute or two they were moving off again, heading in a direction indicated by the creature that had brought them to their present state of being hunted. Neither Tern nor Vivienne had the slightest idea where they were or where they were going. As for Brooking, he was now staggering along in a state of semi-consciousness, firmly in the grip of the Blue Peril. Vivienne, too, though receiving far more considerate treatment, was also the subject of a certain amount of restraint and support. Tern alone was free to go his own way, held only by invisible chains on account of the woman.

Questioned, the monster still refused to tell them where they were going. 'You will see shortly,' was all it would say. 'Be patient, as I have told you before.'

They shivered from the cold, for the abrupt change from the autumn climate of England, bad as that was, was too much; and a considerable amount of snow had recently fallen, making progress difficult if not actually hazardous. By now, all sound of the two fighter planes had faded, the machines having returned to base after fruitless strafing activities.

And then the trees thinned and Tern found himself looking out across a clearing to where a large group of buildings were massed on the far side. There was every sign that the place had been carefully camouflaged from air observation; and when he glimpsed a uniformed figure armed with a submachine gun, he realised that they were looking at some military headquarters.

The monster came to a halt, telling Tern to wait while a plan was formulated. In the icy silence at the fringe of the forest they stood, shivering and watching, most of their curiosity damped by the cold. But there were several aspects of this place that attracted Tern's attention. He could not be sure, but he had a hazy idea that he had heard rumours of such hidden posts from some of his colleagues back in London. If they were right, the monster had brought them to a singularly dangerous spot from which to continue its operations.

Tern glanced obliquely at Vivienne, trying to reassure her with his glance. Their eyes met and held, understanding flowing between them.

'We are ready,' said the monster. 'There is a hidden way of entry to this place; we shall use it to save ourselves trouble. That way, Tern. Hurry, please!' It jerked its hideous head to the trees behind them. 'We must pass round the clearing and approach from the rear,' it added.

Tern grunted, wishing for the thousandth time that he had a gun and could blast this foul creation from the face of the earth. But he started off doggedly again, obedient to the will of their captor. He was only glad that the Blue Peril had not again used its hypnotic influence on him.

During the journey round the edge of the clearing, Tern was able to take better stock of the buildings and the various oddities about their layout. He was particularly curious as to the purpose of several large concrete ramps, the ends of which appeared to be sunk in the fringe of the forest. Heavy entanglements of barbed wire screened them off from the rest of the place.

When he asked the monster for an explanation, the thing only grinned vindictively. 'Again, Tern, you will see!' it said in its shrill, piping tones.

Entry to the main enclosure of the building group was far simpler than Tern had expected. One end of a concealed concrete tunnel opened in the forest about a hundred yards from the buildings. When they first sighted it, a man was standing guard in front of the heavy iron gate that barred all entry to it. But when the monster paused and used its powers, the sentry shouldered his rifle, turned to the gateway, used a key on the lock, and finally slouched off into the woods, where he was last seen lying down with every apparent intention of going to sleep.

Tern glared at the monster. 'So you've

learnt their language?' he said tersely. 'You should take up teaching in your spare time. It'd be more peaceful than this kind of thing.'

'Mockery is not to my taste,' came the cold rejoinder. 'We are now at liberty to enter this secret installation. You will be particularly careful to do exactly as I tell you. Do not fail, for Vivienne's sake!'

'Keep your threats to yourself,' Tern retorted angrily. 'You know you've got me where you want me.'

The tunnel they entered was wide, lit at intervals by electric lights. Every fifteen yards or thereabouts was a deep recess in the wall, and sitting in each was a man, armed like the sentry outside. But now they dozed peacefully, unaware of the power that had lulled him into oblivion on duty.

The floor of the tunnel was gradually sloping upwards, and when it ended a doorway gave access into what appeared to be a large military office. There were clerks working at desks, three women telephonists at a large switchboard, and an officer poring over a big scale map on a table at the far end.

'Make no noise!' ordered the monster in a whisper. 'They will take no notice of us if we do not disturb them.'

'Which way?' muttered Tern helplessly. Four other doors opened off the office.

'The door immediately in front of us now,' came the reply. 'Walk quietly ahead, please. Vivienne will be all right if you do as you are told.'

Tern glanced from side to side as he walked. There were various nameplates on the desks and doors; but although he had little difficulty in guessing at the language they were printed in, they made no sense as far as he was concerned.

Not one of the clerks or other men in the big room even lifted his head as they walked across the floor. Presumably the Blue Peril had lulled their sensibilities and made them ignore the interruption. Tern reflected that it was a most potent accomplishment. For one thing, it saved a lot of bloodshed.

He reached the door opposite and opened it without waiting to be ordered to. Beyond was what was obviously a well-organised radio transmitting room. And even as he entered, an officer in uniform was speaking into a microphone suspended by a cord from the ceiling. The man was sitting at a desk.

'Ah!' The monster's murmured exclamation was pregnant with a sense of achievement and success.

Tern glanced at it sharply. The officer at the desk suddenly stopped speaking and sat back with a jerk. His mouth began to open slackly at sight of the monster that had entered so abruptly into the very heart of secrecy. Then his eyes were rounding with stark terror as he slowly absorbed the frightful apparition in all its fear-provoking ugliness.

The monster gave him little time to act or even shout. With a violent push, it sent Brooking staggering aside to fall in a heap against the wall, stunned again. It did not bother to release Vivienne, but whirled her almost off her feet as it lunged forward towards the desk in a lightning advance. Tern was knocked flying, cursing quietly. But by that time the man at the microphone had received the full force of one of the monster's clenched fists in his face. He fell back in his chair without a sound, his face crushed and mashed beyond recognition, so tremendous had been the striking force of the small, weak-looking fist. Vivienne uttered the beginning of a scream, but the monster silenced her instantly merely by turning his gaze on her eyes.

Tern, who had started a desperate dash to seize what he hoped might be an opportunity of overcoming the creature, was stopped dead in his tracks by the same expedient. He stood there rocking gently to and fro on his feet, staring vacantly at Vivienne.

Then the mental pressure was relaxed and he found that if an opportunity had ever existed, it was gone now. Bitterly, he walked across to the desk and stood by Vivienne's side as she turned her head away from the unpleasant sight of the dead officer.

The monster leant forward and switched off the microphone. Only then did it look at its companions again. There was a frightening smile on its lips. 'We can talk now,' it said. 'We are no longer on the air. Fetch Brooking from over there and plant him in that chair where we can see him all the time. If he shows any signs of being a nuisance, I shall kill him, though I had hoped to save that pleasure for later.'

'You have it all worked out, haven't you?' said Tern.

'Down to the final detail,' came the triumphant reply. 'Now, if you will take a seat over there, I can keep an eye on you without much trouble. Vivienne, you will remain at my side.'

Tern moved away reluctantly, sitting on the edge of a hard wooden chair beside the one into which he had dumped the unconscious scientist. The dead officer was thrust to the floor and forgotten. The monster, still watching Tern with its malignant gaze, took the vacant chair and drew the pendant microphone down to its own level. It switched on, a red light winking on and off on the wall above Tern's head.

Tern would have given anything to have been able to understand the spate of foreign words and phrases that the monster delivered into the mike. Every instinct told him they were dangerous words, probably aimed at the peace of the world; but unless he could understand, he was even more helpless than before.

The delivery into the microphone went on without a break for five or ten minutes. Then the monster switched off and rose to its feet, its fingers still fastened on Vivienne's wrist. 'The scene is set, as you would say, Tern,' it observed. 'We will now go and watch the initial stages of the operation.'

'You devil!' Tern cried. 'What have you done? What have you set in motion?'

'You wish to know too much, my friend. I will tell you this: your own country is in for a rude awakening. Naturally it will retaliate, and the seeds of war will germinate with surprising rapidity. I decided long ago that the best way to wreak my revenge on the human race was to set the nations at one another's throats. What simpler thing than from here, where everything is already prepared for such a strike?'

Tern clenched his fists, advancing on

the monster regardless of his danger. But the monster stayed him before he had covered a yard. 'When will you learn that you cannot attack me, Tern?' it said mildly. 'You could never reach me — and if you did, you could never harm me enough to save Vivienne's life and escape.'

Tern relaxed. He knew he would have to think up some more subtle form of attack than the direct approach and the use of force. But what? The awful implication of what the Blue Peril had just told him was enough to make his brain whirl. He did not even know the manner of the attack to be launched on England. How could he possibly prevent it?

'Come!' ordered the monster more sharply. It thrust Vivienne along at its side, gesturing for Tern to carry Brooking. Then it waited by the door of the radio room — not the door by which they had entered, but a second one across the room.

Tern collected Brooking, a dead weight on his tired shoulders. He began to realise again how desperately weary he was. The added weight of Brooking almost brought him to his knees, but he staggered obstinately out through the door. Beyond lay a short corridor, and at the end of that another door, closed and locked. But there was a key in the lock, and he turned it with one hand, grasping Brooking with the other.

'To the right!' ordered the monster. 'Take no notice of any men you may see; I will control them. Carry on by that wall at the side of the next block.'

Tern could barely find the strength to grunt assent. By burdening him with Brooking, the monster had seriously handicapped him in any attempt at revolt.

They passed only one sentry, a stolid, flat-faced man with dull eyes and unintelligent features. Then they rounded the corner of another block of buildings, and Tern found himself looking out to where the queer-shaped ramps had previously caught his attention. Now they were the scene of terrific activity, with men running this way and that in orderly fashion. Instinctively he came to a halt as the monster and Vivienne came up beside him. The eyes of the monster were blazing with hideous enjoyment.

'They are getting ready!' it said. 'Do you see that? Before long we shall witness the first of many such launchings.'

'What is it?' demanded Tern. He let go of Brooking and let him fall to the ground like a sack of rags. 'What is this cursed place?'

'One of many guided missile launching bases,' came the frightening reply. 'Does that answer your query?'

12

Homeward Bound

'You mean these people are going to let off a rocket aimed at Britain?' blurted Tern. 'You can't let them do it, damn you! The country isn't ready for such an attack! Thousands of innocent people will die, just to satisfy your savage lust for revenge!'

'Precisely, Tern. Millions, not thousands . . . This place can handle a hundred launchings in a few hours. A constant stream of projectiles will rain on London and all your larger cities during the night. You can only see three of the launching ramps from here because of the darkness, but I assure you there are many more along the fringe of the forest.'

Tern suddenly hurled himself on the monster, forgetful of danger, knowing only that somehow these frightful events must be stopped; prevented from ever happening.

He was brought up short by a cry of agonising pain from Vivienne as the Blue Peril jerked at her arm, almost tearing it from its socket. At the same time, the creature turned its eyes full on him in the gloom. They seemed to glow with living fire, paralysing him, crushing his will and making him cower fearfully. Vivienne's cry turned to a sob.

'Don't do it, Tern!' hissed the monster. 'I have not finished with you yet, or I would destroy you completely — as I hope to destroy the whole of your race in time. You are only witnessing the very small beginnings of what will be the most catastrophic and total war ever waged by the countries of the world since the start of time!'

Tern could only shudder uncontrollably. From the corner of his eye, he saw the men by the nearest launching ramp gather round a large articulated lorry that had just drawn up. Resting on it was a long, gleaming pencil-shaped object, the menace of it horribly clear in the patches of light thrown by operating lamps spaced at intervals round the back end of the ramp. The fore end of the projectile was painted bright red for a considerable distance along its length. Streamlined fins projected from the rear, with the circular orifice of the driving unit tucked between them. A heavy mobile crane moved into position. He could hear men shouting orders and the grind of machinery; the whirr of electric motors as the crane swung across and its tackle came to rest above the loaded projectile.

'Don't you realise what you're starting?' Tern muttered. 'I know you're not human, but we are! You can't make us stand by and watch that thing sent off to bring death to people like ourselves! Haven't you a spark of pity in your being?'

He was pleading now; begging for mercy for his fellow men, not so much for himself. He didn't matter now; this was too big. He would willingly sacrifice his own life if he thought there was the slightest chance of stopping this thing, but he was so afraid that it would be a wasted effort; a futile one. And he could not afford to waste his life if there was a chance that sooner or later he could turn the tables.

'It is most interesting,' said the monster quietly. 'I had not expected this backward race to produce such a weapon and handle it with such efficiency. I have no doubt whatever that it will serve its purpose once it is launched. The ones that follow will complete the good work.'

'You fool!' groaned Tern. 'The world only needs a spark to set it off.'

'Exactly, Tern. I am supplying that spark. When I used the radio to issue local orders, I merely informed the men that an unprovoked attack had been made on a number of the country's cities. I spoke on behalf of their leader, giving the necessary orders for immediate retaliatory action. It was simple, and will prove so very effective.'

Tern could only stare in consternation at the busy figures of the men as they loaded the gleaming missile onto its ramp. All sense of his own plight and that of Vivienne was swamped now. Brooking was entirely forgotten — a nonentity; half-crazy when conscious, and a burden when insensible. The fact that they had him to thank for this mounting danger made little difference. In a few minutes, nothing would hold back this ghastly event. And Tern guessed that at other ramps, men were working just as feverishly to do the same awful thing.

So intent were they all on watching proceedings that even the monster failed to notice Brooking when he stirred and opened his eyes. They were wild with insanity by this time; and, if anything, that increased the danger of the man.

The projectile was being lowered slowly and carefully into position now. As Tern watched, it slid gracefully down to the rear of the launching ramp to come to a standstill with its red-painted nose just showing from the barrel-like terminal of the ramp. Tern knew that if any attempt was going to be made to prevent the firing of it, it must be made soon.

And it was then that he became aware of a slight movement behind him. Glancing round, he was horrified to see that Brooking was on his knees. Two yards away a dull-eyed guard stood slackly against the wall, victim of the monster's control. And Brooking had been to his side and now held a submachine gun pointing straight at Vivienne's back. His lips were drawn back in a savage grin. The monster was shielded from Brooking by the body of the woman; but bullets would pass through a body at that short range.

Tern did not wait to think. He yelled and threw himself at Brooking in one blind instant of time. But Brooking gave a lurch and escaped the worst of the impact. In the moment when Tern hit the ground in a sprawl, the machine gun broke into a fiendish chatter of noise. Vivienne screamed. There was a peculiar coughing sound from the Blue Peril. Tern tried to twist round but felt the weight of the scientist's body on top of his own, crushing him down. He heaved and got up on his feet again. Brooking still gripped the gun in his hands, but his face was blank and dead-looking in the semi-darkness. Suddenly his eyes opened wider and wider, his mouth fell open, a terrible expression settled on his features, and the whole of his body crumpled up as if there had been some explosion inside it. Tern knew, then, that the monster had killed him by the very force of its crushing will.

Tern glanced quickly at Vivienne, terrified that he would see her lying dead on the ground, killed by one of Brooking's bullets. But instead she crouched against the wall, her hands over her face.

The Blue Peril swayed unsteadily on its feet. Tern seized the machine gun from Brooking's unresisting grasp, swinging it round towards the monster, meaning to finish what the scientist had started.

But he did not fire, because men were running towards them from the launching ramp, a rifle spat venomously, and further off a machine gun opened up. It dawned on him that they would be lucky to get out of here alive. He ducked as bullets chipped concrete from the wall above his head. Then the guard from whom Brooking had taken the machine gun came to life and dragged at a revolver in his belt. Vivienne cried a warning

— almost too late. Tern swung the gun and pressed the trigger, cutting the sentry down with a burst. At the same time, he shouted to the Blue Peril.

'Stop those others! We can't hold 'em on our own!'

But the monster seemed to be less than its normal self. It leaned back against the wall, its massive head slightly to one side. A trickle of blood ran down from its mouth, and Tern glimpsed a ragged bullet hole in the metal of its torso. Brooking had wounded it.

And all the time the oncoming troops were getting nearer. The air seemed to hum with bullets and shouted orders. If the monster could no longer help them, it was time to go. Tern ran to Vivienne, seizing her arm and dragging her backwards. On the way, he grabbed up the revolver dropped by the dead sentry. Vivienne took it from him, starting to run as he turned and sprayed the vanguard of advancing men. Only the gloom had so far saved them from being killed.

Then the monster seemed to recover a little of its strength. It held out a hand towards Tern. When it spoke, its voice was a shadow of its former shrillness. 'Wait!' it said thinly. 'I can still aid you, but I am injured. Brooking is dead now.'

Tern gritted his teeth. 'For God's sake, come on, then!' he snapped. 'There isn't a moment to lose. Halt 'em, damn you!' He threatened the creature with the gun, holding his fire because there was just a chance that this being could save them.

The monster started moving stiffly, all its old agility gone. Tern saw its weakness and leapt towards it, seizing its arm and dragging it forward. 'Quick!' he gasped, glancing along the wall to where Vivienne was cowering down behind the body of the fallen guard. 'Quick! If we hang about, we're done! Use your brain!'

There was no resistance on the part of the monster. It allowed itself to be guided by Tern; but when the pair of them paused after joining Vivienne and it tried to control the mass of oncoming troops, the effect was disappointingly slight. Within a minute or two of the temporary check effected, the whining of bullets had begun again. They were under fire now from two different flanks, and the situation was getting desperate.

Tern used the machine gun and had the satisfaction of seeing several men fall, but he knew in his heart that the end must come before long. And somehow or other he must prevent that guided missile from ever being launched. Gripping the monster firmly, he sprayed bullets at the enemy with his free hand. Vivienne was taking shots with the revolver. The three of them worked back towards the nearest doorway. This, thought Tern hopefully, was where the Blue Peril might still prove its worth. 'Where's the main control room of this place?' he demanded.

It was curious how passive the monster was now. Wounded, it seemed to have lost its power to terrify; it was almost an object of pity. But it still retained some of its strength. 'Through that door and down the passage beyond,' it said.

Tern fired another burst, staying the advance a little. Vivienne got the door open. They backed through it in a bunch, firing as they went. 'I'll get you out of this and give you another chance to wreak revenge if you do as I ask,' said Tern.

The passage was dark and silent. Outside, the shooting had stopped for want of a target. Tern shot a burst through the closed door, delaying action. At the end of the passage was another door, a stouter one, bolted on the outside. Vivienne got it open and darted through. A man looked up, his face a picture of amazement as he caught sight of her. He was grabbing for a gun when she shot him in the head. And then they were in the control room, a vast, brightly lighted place of switchboards, humming generators and batteries of instrument dials. Tern saw a desk and microphone. That was what he needed more than anything else. He thrust the monster towards it.

'Issue orders to stop the launch!' he grated. As he spoke, he rammed the muzzle of the machine gun in the creature's spine. 'Do as I tell you or I'll fire!'

The monster summoned a smile. 'I never did ask for life,' it said slowly and painfully. 'Strange now that as I stand in danger of losing it, I am ready to bargain to keep it. I trust you, too, Tern. We shall escape from this.'

'Get cracking on the radio!' snapped Tern impatiently. 'You look after us and we'll look after *you* — on our terms!'

'Very well.' It went slowly to the desk and sank into the chair, glancing up at Tern. 'I am to prevent the missile from being launched?'

'Yes!' Tern swung away as the door came open. Vivienne gasped and fired her revolver. Tern's finger tightened on the trigger of the machine gun. The men in the doorway were scattered by the hail of stammering lead. 'Hurry!' shouted Tern to the monster.

The monster seemed to steady itself, gripping the edge of the desk and staring balefully back at him. Then it was talking into the microphone, an unintelligible stream of words. The glass of a window high in the wall shattered. A bullet sang dangerously close to Vivienne's head. Tern swung round and fired from the hip. The body of a man pitched through the broken window. Then Tern was running fast to where a bank of generators was humming quietly at the far end of the control room. He fired into them, wrecking them. While the monster was still talking on the radio, he then destroyed the switchboards, leaving only the one which he thought was connected with the radio transmission.

The monster stopped talking and rose to its feet. 'It is done, Tern. The launching orders are cancelled. I said it was all a mistake that they were to wait for definite orders from higher command. Now we must leave this place at once.'

'You bet!' said Tem grimly. 'If we can!'

The monster indicated another door at the opposite end of the big room. 'Through there,' it said. 'Help me; my legs are losing their strength. We must hurry.'

Tern hesitated for only a second. He had given his word to stand by the Blue Peril, and could not now abandon it. The thing could still serve them in many ways, too.

Through the door was a long corridor, a place of light and shadow. It opened onto a square, with the night sky above.

There were no troops about. Tern wondered why. Then he heard sounds of renewed activity from the direction of the launching ramps and wondered again. Had the monster tricked them?

The three of them ran across the square, heading for a gate in the wall. Before they reached it, a group of men appeared behind them. A bullet snicked Tern's jacket sleeve. He whirled at a cry from Vivienne, firing as he went, stemming the advance. Men were shouting at them now, cursing in a foreign tongue that was meaningless to them. Then they were through the gate and sprinting as fast as they could over open ground.

The Blue Peril made heavy going of it, the sound of its breath horribly laboured. Tern thought it must be dying. Then it stopped in its tracks, seizing his arm. 'What's the matter?' he demanded urgently.

'Half a mile further to the north you will find a small landing ground,' it said. 'It is used by generals and the like when they visit here. There is a ski-equipped plane standing by in a hangar under the trees, a light plane.'

Tern felt a surge of relief. 'Come on, then!' he said more cheerfully. 'We might just make it!'

'You may carry on alone, Tern. I can look after myself from now on. Hurry!'

For answer, Tern grabbed the creature's arm and tried to drag it in the desired direction. But the monster's strength was not all spent. It threw him off and staggered away, breaking into a run as it headed for the launching ramps.

'Let it go!' gasped Vivienne. 'Please, darling!'

'We can't!' he snapped. 'It'll start trouble all the time it's alive!' As he spoke, he levelled the machine gun. But before he could begin to squeeze the trigger, there was a shuddering roar from the nearest launching ramp, and a great gout of flame and smoke. 'My God!' gasped Tern. 'The devil never cancelled his orders after all. It was a trick!'

Vivienne seized his arm. The Blue Peril paused and glanced back over its shoulder. It was almost lost in the gloom by now. 'Run!' it called. 'If you want to save yourselves, run and get away from here. That missile is coming straight down again. I gave the necessary orders!'

'Damn you!' Tern yelled. 'You meant to do some damage, didn't you?' But Vivienne was dragging at him urgently, and he gave in. They ran for all they were worth, catching a last glimpse of the monster as it went on towards the launching ramps, moving more slowly than ever now, sagging weakly at every stride.

They just reached the edge of the forest in time. With an appalling roar and whistling howl, a great fiery shape shot earthwards. The whole of the ground seemed to shiver and rise up in a fountaining gush of fire and debris. Tern and Vivienne flattened themselves to the cold earth, praying silently, battered by the blast and concussion. Earth, snow, and pieces of stone fell and clattered all round them. It seemed to go on for hours, the first explosion of the missile being followed by others as the shock detonated other waiting projectiles.

In a state of semi-consciousness, the two of them crawled further away. Behind them a terrible silence had fallen. No voice was raised either in pain or question; no human being could have lived through the holocaust inflicted on the site by the Blue Peril's action in destroying it. Even the monster itself could not have survived.

Tern reached a wooded crest, looking back at the smoking ruins of the launching site. His arm was round Vivienne's shoulder, holding her close at his side. 'Come on,' he said gently. 'We aren't clear yet, remember.'

In the distance, a train sounded very faintly. Nearer, the rumble of a motor vehicle was audible. Shivering from the intense cold, Tern and Vivienne started off for the landing field. The reign of the Blue Peril was over, but they themselves were in a foreign country, surrounded by hostile forces and innumerable dangers yet to be faced. But they were together . . .

Sure enough, the monster's directions had been correct. Within a few minutes they were standing on the edge of a small clearing plainly used as a landing ground. And it did not take long to locate the light plane and warm it up. Tern said little of the dangers ahead, but his face was grim as he taxied out for a take-off.

The fighters picked them up just before they crossed the coast. Two came at them simultaneously. Only the fact that the plane was amazingly manoeuvrable enabled Tern to avoid the first onslaught of cannon fire. Then began a period of hide-and-seek in the low cloud. Several times they were attacked; and then, when it seemed that they lad at last thrown off pursuit by sheer evasive action, the engine stuttered and died, its fuel exhausted. They were over the sea and Tern had lost his bearings.

'This is it, sweet!' he muttered. 'We've done all we can, I'm afraid. You're not frightened, are you?'

'Not now,' she whispered. 'Not with you. Kiss me.'

Their lips touched in what was to be a farewell caress as the plane began to glide more swiftly down towards the cold, inhospitable waves. Time seemed to hover endlessly. Tern opened his eyes and looked out through the side window, past Vivienne's forehead, thinking hungrily of the life they were soon to end in each other's arms; the life they had barely begun and which had promised to be so full. And now, when the plane struck the water, it would all be finished. There were no parachutes on board, and no chance of rescue even if there had been.

'Aren't those lights?' muttered Vivienne with a sob.

'Lights?' Tern snapped, disengaging himself. 'Where?'

But before she could even point with her hand, he had seen them himself. A little distance to port, he glimpsed the red and green of navigation lights, the glowing portholes of a ship. And there was still time; they still had enough height; the plane was gliding fast but on a level keel.

In an instant Tern had seized the controls again, taken over from Fate. It didn't matter what ship this was, or what country she sailed from; she represented life to their hungry souls.

Vivienne found and fired a Very pistol in the air. Tern flattened out fifty feet above the dark water, gliding swiftly towards the ship so as to land ahead of it.

An answering light soared up from the bridge. Tern could even hear the bellow of the siren in acknowledgement. And then the long, low hull of a rakish destroyer was visible as they streaked by. Next moment they touched, bounced up again, hesitated and finally pancaked on the icy water. The destroyer was fifty yards away, coming up fast. Tern and Vivienne were out of the cabin, clinging to the sinking aircraft by the time a boat was lowered and reached them.

Concentration camp for the rest of our lives, thought Tern sourly. It might have been better to have pranged and be done with it. Then a voice came floating to his ears.

'Blimey, 'Arry, there's a poor perishin' gal as well! 'Ere, mate, catch 'old!' A line was thrown from the boat. Tern grabbed it, and before long he and Vivienne were being helped up the ladder to the deck of an H.M. destroyer engaged on fishery patrol beyond the international limit. Never, thought Tern, had he realised what a blessing the British navy could be.

And then they were homeward bound

for Portsmouth at the close of the patrol. There would be a lot of questions to answer, a lot that might not be believed, perhaps even official trouble to face and overcome; but the main thing was that there was no more Blue Peril, no more Brooking. And the imminent danger to their native land had been staved off.

When Tern went to bed in a narrow bunk after a stiff tot of rum, it was to fall into a deep sleep, not only of sheer exhaustion but of peace, and the knowledge of peace. He and Vivienne were homeward bound, together.

We do hope that you have enjoyed reading this large print book.

Did you know that all of our titles are available for purchase?

We publish a wide range of high quality large print books including:
Romances, Mysteries, Classics
General Fiction
Non Fiction and Westerns

Special interest titles available in large print are:
The Little Oxford Dictionary
Music Book, Song Book
Hymn Book, Service Book

Also available from us courtesy of Oxford University Press:
Young Readers' Dictionary
(large print edition)
Young Readers' Thesaurus
(large print edition)

For further information or a free brochure, please contact us at:
Ulverscroft Large Print Books Ltd.,
The Green, Bradgate Road, Anstey,
Leicester, LE7 7FU, England.
Tel: (00 44) **0116 236 4325**
Fax: (00 44) **0116 234 0205**